The Awakening of Caellaias

Book Three of The Kingdom of Caellaias Series

Mikaelynn Rose

To everyone who has encouraged me to pursue my joy of writing, even through all the ups and downs, life has thrown my way. I appreciate you all more than you could ever know.

And to my husband, who always sticks by my side, no matter what. You're my ride or die and I wouldn't have it any other way. I love you.

Content Warnings

- Sexual content

- Racism

- Mentioned suicide, discovery by child

- Sex trafficking/prostitution

- Mentions of sexual, emotional, and physical abuse

- Voyeurism

- Abduction

Pronunciation Guide

Characters

- Aeros – Air-ohs

- Ahmeira – Ah-meer-uh

- Akantha – Ah-khan-thu

- Amareon – Ah-mare-ee-on

- Amaroc – Am-uh-rock

- Ambrose - Am-brr-ohz

- Anevae – Ana-vay

- Azur – Ah-zoor

- Caevryn Sorric Corvaethen – Cave-rin Sore-ic

Core-vay-TH-en

- Cahir – Cuh-hear

- Calliope – Cuh-lie-oh-pea

- Casimir – Cah-suh-meer

- Cassiel – Cassie-el

- Cordilaen – Core-duh-lane

- Eirian – Eye-ree-an

- Eiri – Eye-ree

- Emrhys Caelthorn – Em-Reese Kale-thorn

- Ilaria – ih-lar-EE-uh

- Kaius – Kai-us

- Koen – Koh-en

- Laeney – Lane-EE

- Maarya – Maur-yuh

- Maeyve – May-v

- Miray – Mih-ray

- Moranna – More-aw-nuh

- Roarc – Row-arc

- Sameera – Suh-meer-uh

- Seliora Vaelisse Corvaethen – Sell-EE-aura Vay-lease Core-vay-TH-en

- Shivani – Shi-vah-knee

Places

- Baeruil – Bay-roo-ill

- Caellaias – Kay-lay-us

- Ceraias – Sir-A-us

- Diathem – Die-ah-TH-em

- Dirsethik – Dur-seh-thick

- Eirvanna – Air-Vanna

- Ellaenea – El-lay-knee-uh

- Feraetheam – Fir-ay-TH-ee-um

- Haelian – Hay-lee-an

- Kaeuil – Kay-U-ill

- Kanlyrae – Can-luh-ray

- Kolathus – Coal-ah-TH-us

- Lamatorre – La-muh-tore

- Maiviraea – My-vuh-ray-uh

- Rilias – Ri-lie-us

- Rilvara – Ril-var-uh

- Tyrkenea – Tear-keh-knee-uh

- Zylithia – Zie-lih-TH-ee-uh

Other

- Orletaylaer – Or-leh-tay-lair

- Thodwyn – Thaw-dwin

- Valaryn – Vuh-lare-in

- Zyelvris – ZIE-el-vr-iss

The Kingdom of Caellaias

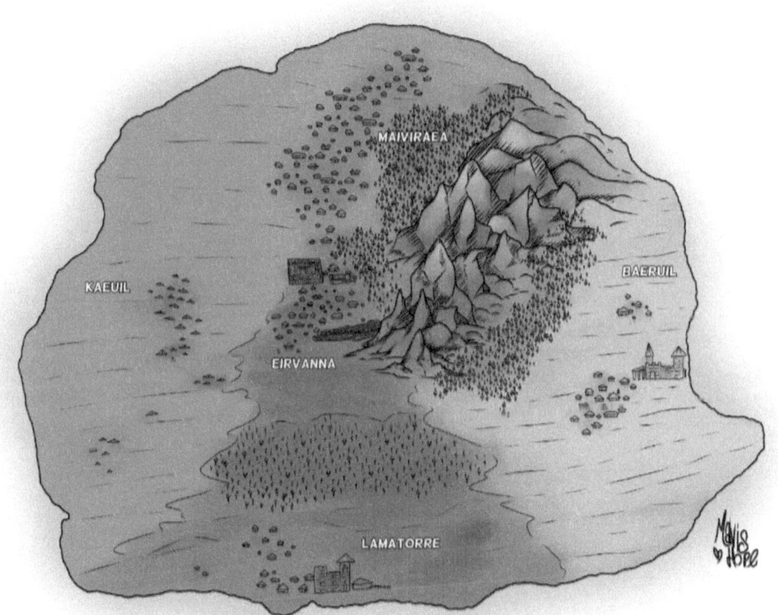

Contents

Chapter One

Anevae

An all-consuming panic overwhelmed me as Emrhys rushed us out of the ballroom. I couldn't believe *he* was in there speaking with my grandfather.

Who's Ambrose? Emrhys asked, his voice full of concern.

Emrhys, get her out and ask questions later, Maeyve snapped.

I couldn't calm my racing heart as we stepped into the hall. My breath bounced off the black and white marble that adorned the walls of the castle. With every inhalation, my anxiety notched up until I wasn't thinking straight. Grabbing Emrhys by the hand, I pulled him up the stairs to my suite.

We're going upstairs, Emrhys told Maeyve. *Try to excuse yourself, find Cassiel, and get up here. She needs all of us right now.*

I'll see what I can do. Since Anevae's parents arrived, she's also been able to call out to Cassiel through their bond.

When Emrhys and I reached the top of the stairs, my lungs felt like they were going to collapse—I couldn't breathe anymore. Emrhys cursed under his breath, scooped me into his arms, and sprinted down the hall to my room. Once inside, he sat me on the couch, kneeling before me.

"What can I do for you right now, princess?"

My mind was so overwhelmed with emotions that a strangled cry left my lips when I tried to respond to him. I was terrified to tell my mates what Ambrose had put me through all those years ago.

Emrhys swept the hair from my face and pulled me onto the floor with him, cradling me in his lap. Maeyve showed up a few minutes later, closing the door lightly behind her. "I was barely able to slip out of the ballroom without drawing any attention to myself, so I wasn't able to look for Cassiel. How can we help you, my love?"

I shook my head as I clung to Emrhys. Out of the three of my mates, he'd become my strength during the hardest of times, so I nuzzled into his neck and let his scent envelop me. My focus drifted to the feel of his arms around me, holding tight to keep me safe and secure.

When he started rocking me, Maeyve rubbed my back in slow, circular motions. The warmth of her calming ability washed over me. With my breathing calming down and my heart bear slowing to a normal pace, the once streaming tears finally stopped free flowing.

Once my body was calmed, it was easier to mend the frayed edges of my thoughts. With the tension easing away from me, I was able to reach out to Cassiel. Not a moment passed where I wasn't thankful for my ability to contact him through our bond, even when it was incomplete.

After a few moments, he appeared in my room, his gaze frantically sweeping the room until he found me and dashed to my side.

"What the hell happened?" he asked, confusion marring his face while he checked me for any possible injuries.

Maeyve sighed. "She's fairly certain she saw one of her exes speaking with the king while she was dancing with Emrhys."

Emrhys' concern seeped through our bond. Pushing away from his grip, I gave him a chaste kiss and rose to my feet. I paced the length of my room, trying to figure out the easiest—and least painful—way to explain the part Ambrose played in my life all those years ago.

I stopped before them, still seated on the floor, took a deep breath, and began, "Ambrose and I started dating when I was about seventeen. Not long after I turned eighteen, he proposed to me. Our relationship lasted for almost four years. I was madly in love with him, and I thought he loved me too, but he..." I paused momentarily to compose myself—I refused to let that monster take any more of my tears. "He began abusing me when we moved away for college. Eiri was the one who helped me escape him by bringing my father in to interfere. He told me he took care of Ambrose several years ago, but now the man from my nightmares is here, and I don't know how I feel about that. I wasn't even aware that he was alive, let alone that he belonged to this realm, but I guess it's not like I knew I belonged here then, either."

Emrhys rose from the floor first, wrapping me in a tight embrace. I wouldn't allow myself to cry again, but my resolve broke when he tried to tell me he was sorry.

A tear rolled down my cheek, and I pushed away from him. Taking his face in my hands, I said, "It's not your fault. You couldn't have known. I thought he was behind me—a part of my past I wouldn't have to deal with ever again. Now that he's here, I'll have to face him again, but you're all with me, and that's what matters the most."

The red of Emrhys' eyes deepened as he looked down at me. "I swear to the gods, if he ever tries to lay so much as a finger on you again, he won't see another day. If he gets anywhere near you, I'll rip his throat out—fuck the consequences."

"I'm right there with Emrhys. I'll rip that motherfucker limb from limb, breaking every bone in his body as I go so he feels every ounce of pain he inflicted upon you and more," Maeyve said as she approached Emrhys and me.

Cassiel, ever the peacekeeper, shifted uncomfortably. "If I catch him, I'll just bring him to one of these two and let them do the dirty work. The less blood on my hands, the better."

A smile crept across my face. "I love you all so very much. Please never forget that."

Maeyve wrapped her arms around my midsection and nuzzled into my hair before whispering, "I love you, too, Anevae. Do we have to leave this room, though? I don't want to go back down to the ballroom. When your other grandfather gets here, I fear the king will have him sit at the same table as your father and me."

Letting go of Emrhys, I faced Maeyve. "Everything will be okay, sweetheart. But if something doesn't seem right, let Em and me know through the bond."

With a nod, she pulled me into her and kissed me deeply. Then I kissed my men, fixed my makeup, and we made our way back to the ball.

The announcer didn't reintroduce me when I entered the ballroom, but the crowd gave me a wide berth, nonetheless. Emrhys escorted me as he was supposed to, while Maeyve and Cassiel came in separately. Suspicions would rise if we were all seen together, and I wasn't willing to let that happen.

When I got back to my seat, Ambrose was gone, but all three of my family members on the dais had their eyes on me.

"Is everything alright?" the king asked as I ascended the stairs.

"I apologize, Grandfather. I went to my suite so I could adjust my hair. It was falling in my face, and I kept tripping over Emrhys' feet. I know I'm clumsy, but my hair obstructing my view wasn't helping."

"Well, I am glad that you were able to remedy the problem swiftly."

"Thank you, Grandfather. I hope I didn't miss anything important."

"Actually, there is someone I would like you to meet."

My heart stopped. I knew he was going to introduce Ambrose and me to each other, but I was dreading it. I wasn't sure I could keep my anxiety under control without one of my mates, but I had to try. Plastering a fake smile on my face, I said, "Of course, Grandfather."

He rose from his seat and approached me, holding out his hand. Begrudgingly, I took it and followed him to the opposite side of the dais from where Emrhys and Maeyve were. Two other guards allowed us to pass them, and a table similar to the one my father sat at was before us. Ambrose sat with his back to us, oblivious that we were approaching, until someone seated across from him stood to bow. Ambrose rose from his chair quickly and spun to bow himself.

"As you were, gentleman," my grandfather said.

When Ambrose stood, he whispered his thanks to the king and looked directly at me. A lump lodged itself in my throat as I met his gaze. But he wasn't quite as I'd recalled. The Ambrose I knew had two green eyes, while the man before me had one eye identical to the one I remembered, and the other was a beautiful honey color.

"Who is this you have with you, Your Majesty?" asked the familiar, deep voice of my nightmares.

My grandfather looked at me with a wide smile on his face. "This is my granddaughter, Anevae. Anevae, this is Amareon. His father is the lord of Eirvanna, so you will see him around often."

Confusion swirled in my mind. Amareon? Was he using a false name in front of my grandfather?

Trying to keep my voice level, I said, "It's a pleasure to meet you, Amareon."

He bowed his head and said, "The pleasure is all mine, Your Highness. I must say, you have a very beautiful name." Then he grasped my hand and brought it to his lips, gently kissing my knuckles. Tingles shot up my arm, and it took everything in me not to yank my hand from his grasp. There was no way I was feeling what I thought I'd felt from him.

When Amareon released my hand, I turned back to the king. "Grandfather, I need some water. May I return to the dais?"

"Of course you may, darling. I shall return in a few moments."

I tried not to move back to my seat too fast, but I was panicking again. *I don't know who that is, but I'm fairly certain he's not Ambrose,* I said to my mates.

Confusion rippled through the bond, and Maeyve asked, *Why do you say that?*

My eyes met hers as I sat and let out a shaky breath. *Something about this man is... different than with Ambrose. While he may look exactly the same, this man has one green eye and one that's honey colored. Ambrose's eyes were both green. And when this man kissed my knuckles, the contact with his skin sent tingles up my arm. That never happened with Ambrose. Then, when my grandfather introduced us, he said this man's name is Amareon. The man could be lying, but it seems like my grandfather knows him well. Needless to say, I really don't think that's Ambrose.* Maeyve and Emrhys were quiet, which set me on edge. *Someone say something, please?*

I'm grasping at straws here, but what if that is Ambrose over there, and someone glamoured themselves to look like him in the human realm? Maybe when you guys touched before, your magic was so suppressed, the mate bond didn't call to you. Did your grandfather say anything else about him while you were over there? Emrhys asked.

I settled back into my seat. *I'm fairly certain I heard him say that Amareon's father is the lord of Eirvanna.*

Out of my periphery, Emrhys shifted his stance. *Lord Koen. I can do some investigating. I've met many of the lords and ladies of the kingdom, but it's rare they bring their whole families to these gatherings. There's got to be a reason the lord would bring his son to this ball, and the king wanted to introduce you to him. Don't worry, princess; we've got you.*

Maeyve's unease flooded the bond. *I, uh, hate to interrupt, but we have a problem. Roarc has spotted someone entering the ballroom who has him on the edge of his seat. But I can't see who it could be from where I'm sitting.*

I snuck a glance at my mom beside me. She'd clenched her teeth as she stared at the entryway to the ballroom.

Trumpets sounded, drawing everyone's attention to the new arrival. The man introducing the influential figures as they entered the ballroom cleared his throat and said, "Presenting Amaroc Ravenheart, Lord of Southern Maiviraea."

When the guards moved, I got a good look at my paternal grandfather for the first time. He wasn't an overly tall man, probably about five feet ten inches tall with a muscular build. The way he wore his crimson hair was identical to the way my dad had worn his for my entire childhood. His pale blue eyes swept across the table as he approached the dais, briefly pausing on me and then Eiri. Seemingly dissatisfied, his gaze drifted to the table where my dad and Maeyve sat.

I held my breath, praying that his focus was on my dad, not Maeyve. Thankfully, he stopped at the bottom of the dais and addressed my other grandfather, bowing deeply. "King Casimir, thank you for the invitation to your celebration. I am pleased that our *children* have finally returned home. It's been far too long. The girls seated beside Cordilaen must be our granddaughters."

"Thank you for joining us, Amaroc. You are correct, the girls are our granddaughters. They are beautiful, are they not? I was certain you would be interested in seeing them for yourself. Oh, and your son, since it has been so long."

"Our granddaughters are very beautiful indeed. I see the eldest inherited her father's hair color and eyes. Is she the one you've said is a troublemaker thus far?"

King Casimir let out a breathy laugh. "That she is. Her sister has been an absolute delight. She hasn't given me any trouble yet."

"Splendid. I do look forward to getting to know them. We've already missed so much of their lives."

"We have, but they are still very young, so we have plenty of time."

Lord Amaroc met my gaze and gave me a toothy grin that was all wrong. It made me want to shrivel into myself and disappear. Then he gasped. "Ah. Before I forget, I have brought the madam from Western Maiviraea you requested to take care of the... mutt you mentioned."

My heart sank into my stomach as Lord Amaroc stepped to the side, and a woman approached the dais. She was gorgeous in a scary sort of way. Her full lips curved into a menacing smile when her dull, nearly colorless eyes landed on Maeyve. Her lithe body trembled with... excitement?

Maeyve's terror trickled through the bond, sending a chill through my body, and I shot to my feet, slamming my fist down on the table before me. "*NO!* She does *NOT* belong to you anymore. If you lay a finger on her, I will k—"

King Casimir shoved my mom out of the way and gripped my chin, electricity dancing across my skin. His voice came out as a low hiss. "That is *not* your decision. It is mine and mine alone. Do you think I don't know what you're up to? As if I haven't seen the *mark* on your neck. It's disgusting. I don't know how it happened, but she will not stay here, and I will have the bond broken in the near future. You can blame your mother for what is to come. If she had done her duty and married Lord Koen as I had instructed all those years ago, this would *not* be happening. Now, you need to *sit the fuck down* and shut up. Do you understand?"

My nostrils flared as I fought the urge to cry. When his grip on my jaw tightened, I forced myself to nod. He threw me back into my chair without warning and returned to his own. The ice in my veins had solidified, and I couldn't move again.

Emrhys was panicking on the stairs, but there was nothing he could do as Madam Tanith strode over to where Maeyve sat and yanked her out of her chair. Tears spilled down Maeyve's cheeks, but she didn't fight the madam. I wasn't sure if she knew it wouldn't do her any good or if she didn't want me to get into any more trouble than I already was. Either way, the weight of her terror mounted and threatened to suffocate me through our bond.

I'm sorry, my love. This isn't the end. We will get you out of there again, even if we have to kill the madam to do so. I love you.

Once Madam Tanith and Maeyve were out of sight, everyone went back to what they were doing.

But it seemed Lord Amaroc wasn't done. "Now that the mutt is taken care of, what would you like done with my son?"

A sinister grin spread across King Casimir's lips. "He can stay. For now. I believe it is important to teach lessons when necessary; he and my daughter desperately need one."

"As you wish, Your Majesty. I would love to sit and speak with him for a while. If that is okay?"

"Absolutely, Amaroc. I will have one of the servants fetch you some food. I apologize for my invitation being sent at the last minute; I didn't know when our *children* would grace us with their presence."

"That is much appreciated, Your Majesty. And never mind the lateness of the invitation."

King Casimir flagged down a servant as he'd promised when Amaroc headed for the table my dad sat at. Then the king settled back into his seat, watching over his subjects. Everyone around us had resumed as normal, but tension hung heavy around my family.

When I couldn't handle it anymore, I asked, "Grandfather, may I retire to my room for the evening? I am quite tired. It has been a long day."

"If you leave this room, you are to go directly to your suite with no detours. You will *not* go after that mutt. She is long gone by now. Emrhys, did you hear that?"

"Yes, Your Majesty. I will ensure she goes directly to her room."

"Perfect. Anevae, do not cause a scene when you leave. You have been testing my patience. Now, be off, and let me enjoy my celebration," the king hissed.

I wanted to be alone, away from all the prying eyes, so I had no problem following his orders. The walk to my room was torture; my body was weak, and my mind fractured. Maeyve was gone. I didn't know when I'd see her again, which scared me. The moment I stepped foot inside my room, I collapsed on the floor.

Chapter Two

Emrhys

Not even one step into the room, Anevae collapsed. I threw the door shut behind me and scooped her up before she could hit the floor. Cradling her to my chest, I strode over to the bed, climbed on, and held her tightly as she wept.

Madam Tanith took our mate from us with the help of the king and Lord Amaroc. I had every intention of making every single person involved pay for the pain and suffering they inflicted on my mates. The whole situation was so surreal, but the further Maeyve got from the castle, the more the ache in my chest grew, and reality began to settle in. I wasn't sure how we'd be able to get her back, but I knew we'd do it if it were the absolute last thing we did. Over the next few weeks, the king would keep close tabs on Anevae, wanting to make sure she wouldn't go after Maeyve, so we'd have to be even more careful than we had already been. Regardless of our safeguards, it wasn't enough to protect Maeyve.

Maeyve and Anevae had made no attempts to cover their marks when they first arrived at Castle Rilvara, and I couldn't help but wonder how long the king had known about their mating. Either way, he had allowed Maeyve to stay, which surprised the fuck out of me. I was glad he did; I was just shocked he hadn't taken action sooner.

Cassiel's sudden arrival startled me out of my thoughts, and I instinctively clutched Anevae closer to my chest. He leaped on the bed, looking Anevae over. Some of the tension left my body knowing he was there, but the way he looked at her made me think he'd heard, if not actually seen firsthand, what happened in the ballroom.

He stroked her hair and whispered, "I'm so sorry, sweetheart. We'll get her back."

Her grip on my shirt tightened until I was sure she'd rip the fabric, and she cried harder. Unable to speak, she connected with me through our bond. *This is all my fault. I should've made her stay in the human realm. She was so afraid this would happen, and I couldn't do anything to stop it, even though I promised time and time again that she'd be safe.*

Maeyve spoke to us through the shared bond, and my shoulders sagged in relief. *It's not your fault, Anevae. When I brought you into Caellaias, I came knowing someone could report my presence to Madam Tanith. But when it didn't happen right away, I let my guard down and assumed we were safe. I'll find another way out of the brothel; the madam can't keep me locked up forever.*

Sadness flooded our bond, but I couldn't tell who it was coming from. I had to do something. *Do you know where you are? Maybe I can find someone to intercept the carriage and bring you back. Or maybe Cassiel can convey himself to you.*

I don't think that's going to work, Em. I'm not entirely sure where we're at, and it's gotten so dark I can't see anything worthwhile. My eyes in human form are nowhere near as good as they are in my fox form. Not to mention, you guys can't risk anything. Don't come after me. I'll find a way back as soon as possible.

The tears flowing down Anevae's cheeks had slowed, but she still held onto me for dear life. Hearing Maeyve speak to us through the bond gave Anevae a small sense of relief, but I knew she was still blaming herself for what happened, no matter what Maeyve said.

When she lifted her head, she tried to push away from me, but I tipped her chin up to look at me. "Unless you feel sick or need to use the bathroom, you are *not* leaving my lap right now. And until Maeyve is back with us, you won't be leaving my sight again. It's only a matter of time before your grandfather discovers you and I have also mated. When that happens, I'm as good as dead."

Her eyes widened. "I-I... No. We're finding Maeyve and leaving Caellaias as soon as possible. I've already failed to keep my promises to Maeyve once, and I can't fail you, too."

I dropped my forehead to hers. "Maeyve knew what she was getting herself into when she came to Caellaias with you. Your mate bond may have thrown a wrench into things, but she knew the madam could come for her at any point, and she came anyway. I've accepted what I'm facing. When I touched you that first day outside the castle, and felt the tingles run through my body, I knew I couldn't stay away from you. I hoped things would change once you and Eirian got settled—that your grandfather would change my station or something to keep me away from you—but then he assigned me to be your guard. I tried to fight it, but gods, I wanted you so fucking bad. How couldn't I? You're so gods damned beautiful and perfect in every single way, and while I didn't understand it, you were supposed to be mine. The day you invited me into your bedroom and mated with me will forever be one of the best days of my life. I chose you, and so did Maeyve. You haven't failed *anyone*, princess. Not in the least. If anything, you've given my life purpose again."

Her brilliant blue eyes flicked over my face as a tear slid down her cheek. "I'm sorry," she whispered.

Sweeping away the tear, I kissed her cheek. "You don't need to apologize for anything. Maeyve made her choices, and so have I... I love you, Anevae."

Eyes wide, her mouth popped open on a sharp inhale. I swore her heart skipped a beat, which almost made mine come to an abrupt stop.

I wasn't sure what I expected, but this wasn't it. Another tear slid down her cheek as she stared at me.

I wiped away the tears and pulled her back against my chest. "You don't have to say anything right now. Just... rest, please."

Cassiel settled in beside me, continuing to stroke Anevae's hair until we all fell asleep.

❦ ❦ ❦

A few hours later, I woke up to Anevae attempting to climb off my lap. I wrapped my arms tighter around her, pulling her back against my chest. "Where do you think you're sneaking off to?"

"Em, I have to use the bathroom and change out of this gown. Go back to sleep, please."

"I know you want some privacy, so I'll grab you a nightgown while you use the bathroom, but I'm not letting you out of my sight unless I'm asleep. Even then, I'm not letting you out of arm's reach."

With a quick nod, she disappeared behind the privacy screen, and I opened the armoire. Maeyve's vanilla and berry scent permeated the air. I grabbed one of her shirts, brought it to my nose, and inhaled her intoxicating scent. My heart ached for her even though it'd been less than twelve hours since the madam took her from us. I let myself bask in Maeyve's scent for a few moments before I put the shirt back and found a nightgown for Anevae.

Anevae had returned to the bed, waiting for me. "Will you please help me get out of this dress? Maeyve normally unlaces the corset for me. It's hard to do on my own."

"Of course. Come here, princess."

She approached and turned away from me. As I swept her hair over her shoulder, my fingers skimmed across her neck, sending shivers through her whole body. The effect my touch had on her brought a smile to my face.

"Hold the top up for me, please. We can't have you giving the angel a free show if he wakes up," I teased, trying to lighten the mood a bit.

As she held onto the fabric, Anevae let out a small laugh, and the ache in my chest eased ever so slightly. I pulled on one of the satin ribbons, untying the bow, and worked to loosen each section without messing up the laces. The dresses her grandfather had made for her were one of her favorite things about the realm. Growing up in a predominantly female household, I helped with many corsets over the years, and I made quick work of the laces.

When I was done, I grabbed her nightgown and stepped in front of her. "You can let go. We'll get this nightgown on you, and then we're crawling back in that bed so you can get some more rest. It's still the middle of the night."

As I helped her into her nightgown, she frowned and looked me up and down. "What about you? You should get comfortable, too."

"I'm fine for now, princess."

"Well, at least take your gear off. I'm sure you have some undergarments underneath."

I rolled my eyes. "You won't give up, will you?"

"No. I want you to be comfortable."

Shaking my head, I said, "I'm fine. I'll take my shoes off, but I don't want you to be without me right now. You matter to me more than my comfort."

"And you matter more to me than my being alone right now. Please, just get comfortable. Cassiel is here if you need to go to your room for anything."

"If someone finds me in bed with you, almost completely undressed, they'll drag me to the king first and ask questions later."

Crossing her arms over her chest, she pursed her lips. "Lock the damn door. If someone tries to come in, it'll wake one, if not all, of us up. Then you'll have time to get out of bed, get dressed, and act as if nothing happened thanks to your super speed."

"Fine," I hissed as I kicked my boots off and stripped down to my underwear, laying them nearby so I wouldn't be struggling to find them if something were to happen. "Happy?"

"Very. Let's wake up Cassiel so he can get comfortable too, and then we'll all be able to get back to sleep."

Cassiel sat up in bed, shirtless. "I already took the liberty of doing so when you guys got up. Emrhys, listen to our girl and lock the door. Anevae, get up here and cuddle with me. The vampire can't steal you all the time."

"I'm not trying to steal her all the time. The further Maeyve gets from the castle, the more my chest aches. Anevae's presence is the only thing that brings me comfort right now," I snapped.

Anevae placed a hand on my arm as she approached me. Getting up on her tiptoes, she gave me a quick kiss. "It's okay, baby. Let's get the door locked and lie down. Tomorrow, we can deal with everything. Tonight, we need our rest."

I dropped my forehead to hers and whispered, "It already hurts so much, and I'm sure they haven't even reached Maiviraea yet. I don't know how we're going to manage it. It's going to be hard to walk out there in the morning and hide the pain I'm in."

"We'll just have to take things one day at a time. We don't have to hide the pain all the time, but we can't jump too far ahead right now, either."

"You're right. Get up in bed and snuggle with your angel. I'll join you both shortly."

Moving her hands to cup my cheeks, she pulled me in for a deep kiss before making her way to the bed. I headed for the door so I didn't have to watch her cuddle up to Cassiel. It's not that I didn't like the angel, but we didn't have that kind of connection. Part of me wanted to run away from the whole situation—let them have the night to themselves while I wallowed in my own self pity and thought of every plan in the book to get our mate back—but Anevae made it clear she wanted me to be with her tonight, too, so I climbed up behind her after locking the door.

I tried to keep my distance, but she reached for me and pulled me in closer. She laced our fingers together and let out a contented sigh. It wasn't long before her breathing evened and she fell into a deep sleep.

The next morning, a light tap on the shoulder startled me awake. Going on the defense, I sprang to my feet, barely holding back a hiss, and came face to face with Cassiel.

"Fuck. Don't do that when I'm already on edge," I muttered.

"I was trying not to wake Anevae, but Maarya will be here soon with Anevae's breakfast. That means I need to get out of here, and you need to get dressed. I have absolutely no reason to be in Anevae's room, but you can at least hang out on the couch and say you were checking on her, or she had a rough night last night, so you stayed to make sure she was okay. If you just want to avoid her altogether, I can take you down to the training room so you can go back to your room without drawing any suspicions."

"I'd rather get dressed and stay here, thanks. I don't like the idea of being conveyed. If I can help it, my feet will stay firmly on the ground for the rest of my life."

A smile crept across Cassiel's face. "One day, I'll get you to try it out. It's a lot of fun."

"Says the one who has the power. There are too many unknowns for me to be comfortable in the least. Like I said before, my feet are staying firmly on the ground."

With a shrug, he leaned over to kiss Anevae's cheek. Then, he said, "See you both soon," and disappeared.

After throwing my clothes back on, I unlocked the door and returned to the bed to wake Anevae. She was still dead asleep, so it took a few minutes to rouse her. When I did, she rolled over onto her back and stretched.

"Morning, princess. Maarya will be here soon with your breakfast, and then we'll need to head to your lessons with Cassiel."

When I mentioned the angel, she looked around for him.

I lightly caressed her cheek. "He left about ten minutes ago, but not before kissing you on your cheek. We're trying to be as careful as possible with who's in your company at all times. His being near you outside of your lessons will draw a lot of attention, which we can't have. If someone were to find him with you in your bed, it would be disastrous—maybe even worse than if I were to be found in your bed. My being inside your room is even pushing it right now, but I know you need me. I'll stay with you until I hear Maarya coming down the hall. I think we've got some time, but you'll need to get up soon."

Anevae covered my hand with hers and let out a sigh. "Thank you, Em. Have you tried to contact Maeyve since last night?"

"I haven't been up much longer than you have, so I haven't had time to try. We can try again in a bit. It's still early, and she may be sleeping."

"But what if she's not?"

I took a deep breath as I leaned over to kiss her forehead. "We still need to take care of you. Our mate would kick my ass if she thought I wasn't putting your needs ahead of finding her. This isn't her first time with Madam Tanith. She knows what to expect."

Tears welled in Anevae's eyes. "But it's been over fifty years since she was there. Things may have changed. The people there may have changed. The madam's tactics may have changed. What if she's walking into a death trap?"

Hearing the possibilities had me grinding my teeth. "Princess, stop. It kills me just as much as it does you to think about our mate being subject to the one place she feared returning to, but we can't go after her without a well-thought-out plan, either. Your grandfather will be keeping a close eye on you for a bit, and we have to lie low until he eases off. I don't like it any better than you do, but our mate is strong. We *will* get her out of there, I promise."

"I'm scared. I don't know what the madam will do to her, and I'm terrified of how she'll come out of that place."

The clacking of heels echoed down the hall, indicating Maarya would be at Anevae's room shortly. I muttered a curse under my breath. "Maarya is almost here. I'm going to step into the hallway until she leaves."

Anevae gave me a curt nod, and I hurried to the door. With a deep breath, I tried to rebuild the facade of a guard not attached to their charge, one who wasn't hurting because one of his mates was in an entirely different territory. When I stepped into the hall, Maarya approached, giving me a skeptical look.

The door clicked shut behind me, and I crossed my arms over my chest. "She had a rough night, rightfully so. I just came by to check on her and make sure she hadn't tried to escape."

The faerie before me shifted uneasily on her feet, and her purple wings drooped behind her. "That was kind of you. I'm just here to drop off her breakfast, per usual. May I?" she asked, gesturing toward the door.

"Of course. She's likely still resting; I just wanted to warn you about her state."

Without another word, she breezed past me, into the room, and set the tray on the table. Then, she turned toward the bed and opened her mouth as if she wanted to say something to Anevae, but she thought better of it and stomped back out into the hallway. As soon as she was out of sight, I joined Anevae to help prepare her for the day.

Chapter Three

Anevae

The first day after Madam Tanith took Maeyve back to the brothel was agonizing, but I managed to make it through mostly unscathed. My parents joined us for dinner that night, forcing Eirian to move further down the table, away from our grandfather, which irritated her to no end. Once my mom and I arrived, she was pushed further down the king's list of favorites. But I had no sympathy for her. This was all her fault, anyway.

That night, Cassiel and Emrhys slept with me again. They were the only comfort I had when the ache in my chest morphed into a searing pain that shot through my whole body. Neither of them asked questions—especially Emrhys, because he felt it too—as they sandwiched me between them and finally lulled me to sleep.

I woke the next morning to Cassiel climbing out of bed. Rolling over, I reached for his hand and asked, "Where are you going?"

He squeezed my hand and gave me a half smile. "I was going to wake Emrhys. It's almost time for breakfast, so I have to go, and he needs to get dressed before Maarya arrives. You'll see me in a bit for your lessons, okay?"

My vision blurred. I had to swallow a lump in my throat and blink back my tears as I nodded and loosened my grip on his hand. Instead of releasing me, he pulled me into his arms and held me. I wrapped my arms around his neck and couldn't stop the tears that streamed down my cheeks. He sat back on the bed and held me, pressing the occasional kiss to my temple or cheek, while I sobbed.

After a few minutes, and some calming breaths, I whispered, "I have to get her out of there, Cass. Who knows what the madam is doing to her—what she's going through? I can't stand the thought of it and, selfishly, I need her. Being so far from her hurts like hell, and I'm sure it hurts her just as much. We can't live like this."

Firm hands wrapped around my middle and eased me from Cassiel's arms. "It'll be okay, princess. Come, lie back down with me for a moment. Cass has to get back to his room before Maarya gets here." Needing the comfort, I settled against Emrhys' fully clothed body, and he laid us down.

Cassiel leaned over and caressed my cheek. Against my lips, he whispered, "I'll see you soon. I love you." Then, he kissed me lightly, and he was gone.

"I love you, too," I whispered to the empty air.

After breakfast, I dressed and went with Emrhys to the training room as usual. Thankfully, Cassiel hadn't tried to push me to do much, but I still wanted to work on harnessing my magic. I was pretty proficient with my electrokinesis, and had recently begun working with my glamour magic—which was proving to be pretty tricky to harness. Since my mom was at the castle, I contemplated asking her for help, but I hesitated because I wasn't ready to have a conversation with her yet.

"Hello, sweetheart. You look beautiful, as always. How are you feeling?" Cassiel asked as we entered the room.

I shrugged my shoulders. "Still like shit, knowing my mate is gone because of me and I can't fucking get her back."

Then I headed straight for the wall of mirrors. Meditation at the beginning of my lessons had become the norm for me. It helped me feel more connected to my magic.

Just as I was about to brush past Cassiel, he grabbed my arm. "Anevae. Come here, baby."

"Let me go, please. I want to just focus on my meditation," I whispered.

"Cass, don't push her," Emrhys said as he strolled up behind me.

With a sigh, Cassiel let go of my arm, but as I stepped away from him, he murmured, "Moping won't bring her back."

Spinning on the spot, I stepped into his space, anger mounting in my body, which had my magic surfacing. "Do you really think I want to be moping around? It's already been two fucking days since that bitch took her. I am *hurting,* Cassiel. I fucking told you that this morning, and it's only getting worse as time goes on. Not to mention, I have to be careful because my grandfather is watching and waiting to see what I do."

The corners of his mouth turned down. "I'm sorry. That's not how I meant it to sound."

Emrhys let out a menacing laugh as he approached Cassiel and patted his chest. "Stop while you're ahead, big guy. She's seconds from frying you from the inside out. Princess, you know he means well; he just doesn't completely understand how you're feeling. I know it hurts—it hurts more than I can explain—but we have to focus on something other than the pain. Working on any sort of plan may help us even a little."

Their words settled in, and I stood down. They were both right. I knew Maeyve was strong and capable of getting herself out, but we couldn't sit around and wait, no matter how much she begged us; we had to do something. Emrhys was hurting too, but he was still putting my needs first. Cassiel wanted to help, not only because he knew how much Maeyve meant to me, but because he could sense how much I was suffering.

When the electricity around me dissipated, Emrhys wrapped me in his arms, whispering his reassurances as he walked me over to the wall of mirrors. A few feet away, I stopped him and held my hand out to Cassiel.

"I'm sorry, Cass. I know you're just trying to help; I'm just overly sensitive when it comes to her absence. Even though it hurt to hear the words, I needed the wake-up call. If there's something—anything—we can do, we need to do it. She would've immediately been developing a plan to find any of us if she were in our shoes. Let's meditate, and then we can talk some more. Deal?"

With a nod, he grabbed my hand, sending comforting tingles through my body, and we continued to the mirrors. When I sat, I expected Emrhys to wander off as he usually did, but he surprised me by plopping down next to me. Even Cassiel stopped in his tracks and stared at Emrhys.

"Am I not allowed to join you guys?" Emrhys asked.

"I, uh, I mean, sure. Why not? You just..." Cassiel trailed off, still stunned.

Looking between the two, a smile crept across my lips. "I'd love for you to join us, Em. We're just not used to it. Thank you."

"I want to support you in any way I can. I could also use a moment to regroup. My mind has been all over recently," Emrhys said.

Leaning over, I grabbed his shirt and pulled him to me, kissing him deeply. When we parted, I said, "I love you so much. Maeyve and I are so lucky to have you."

After we were all settled again, I closed my eyes and took a deep breath. Then I began the process of relaxing my entire body. As each muscle relaxed, my magic flowed into the area, waiting to be called to the surface. Electricity hummed through me when I acknowledged my electrokinesis, but I pushed it to the side for now. I focused on calling forth my glamour magic. I'd only been able to access it a handful of times since I started working with my magic, but I was getting more familiar with the feel of it coursing through me. Reaching for it sent a light breeze skittering across my skin, and every time I felt it, my confidence increased. Glamour magic was the most challenging magic to harness.

When the desired breeze swept through my arms, I focused on it until my hands began to feel cold. Without opening my eyes, I leaned forward and placed my hand on the floor, imagining grass sprouting beneath it. As I focused, the scent of freshly cut grass filled my nostrils. Twin gasps sounded from beside me, and my eyes flew open to make sure everything was okay.

All the air left my lungs when I focused on the mirrors before me. The entire floor in the training room had transformed into a grassy field. I shifted my hand on the ground through the strands of the grass that tickled the palm of my hand. Grabbing a strand, I rubbed it between my fingers. Its softness reminded me of the times my sister and I spent outside as children, rolling down the hill in our backyard. Tears prickled in my eyes, and I raised my hand to wipe them away, breaking my contact with the ground.

When the chill in my hands disappeared, the illusion faded, and I allowed myself a moment to cry. I hadn't realized quite how much I missed the life I had until that moment. Things were so much simpler back when I was just a normal human child—I wasn't anyone special or different compared to other kids. In Caellaias, I couldn't say the same.

With a deep breath, I refocused on my meditation until I was calm again. Normally, using too much of my magic would drain me, but this time I didn't feel tired. When I reopened my eyes, Cassiel and

Emrhys were staring at me, eyes wide, but also on edge in case I'd managed to use too much magic again.

"I'm fine," I said, looking between them.

"That was... incredible," Cassiel whispered.

"It looked—and felt—real," I said.

Still stunned, Cassiel asked, "How did you do it? What did it feel like? I've never met anyone with glamour magic, so I know little about it."

Emrhys and Cassiel listened with rapt attention, barely blinking, while I told them about how I conjured the illusion. The smile on my face was plastered in place, thanks to the pride and excitement lingering in my chest. Cassiel smiled, eyes shining. "I need to do more research on this magic. Maybe while you're at dinner, I can go to Baeruil."

"Since it's a fae royal power, wouldn't it make more sense to look in the library here?" Emrhys asked.

Cassiel thought about it for a moment. "The angels keep a record of nearly everything, so it's basically second nature for me to go to Baeruil when researching something. It wouldn't hurt to look at the library here, though. Just in case they have something that didn't make it to Baeruil. Anyway... how do you feel, sweetheart?"

"I feel fine, actually. I hardly feel like I did anything, even though it looked so intricate," I said, meeting his teal gaze.

His lips parted on a beautiful smile that warmed my aching heart. "You're absolutely remarkable—unlike anyone I've ever met before. And I've been alive for quite a long time. There was a reason the gods or whoever it was chose you to unite this kingdom. I honestly can't wait to see all you're capable of and everything you do for this realm."

My cheeks heated at his praise, and I was unsure how to respond to that, especially since I was still having a hard time believing the prophecy was about me. "You're too sweet. I still have a way to go before I can help anyone. Even myself."

Cassiel rose from his cushion and offered me his hand. "Now that your mind is a little clearer, let's start figuring some things out. Shall we?"

I didn't let another thought pass through my mind before I nodded and took his hand, rising from the floor, and directly into the arms of my sweet angel.

"Thank you, Cassiel," I whispered against his chest. "I love you."

He kissed the top of my head before resting his cheek against my hair. "I love you, too."

We stood there for several moments before I finally pushed at his chest, and he let me go. Standing on my tiptoes, I brushed my lips against his in a gentle kiss. Cassiel tangled his hand in my hair and deepened the kiss. I couldn't help but part my lips and let our tongues tangle, the hunger for him to consume me taking over.

When we finally parted for breath, I placed both hands on his chest. "As much as I want to keep kissing you, Maeyve needs us."

Cassiel kissed my forehead and flashed me another smile. "You're such a selfless woman. We're all so lucky to have you."

"I have my moments."

As I stepped back, another pair of hands landed on my hips. Emrhys' deep voice rumbled in my ear, "You came to this realm all because you wanted to save your sister, even though you feared what you'd find. Then, you stayed for weeks, even though you found out she lied. Just one of those things would have broken a lesser woman, but you pushed through. Seems pretty selfless to me."

I leaned back against Emrhys. "You didn't see the panic attacks I had before coming here. I didn't come after her right away because I literally couldn't; I was so scared. *You* scared me and I also had no idea the state in which I would find my sister."

Emrhys turned me to face him. "But you pushed yourself past that *for your sister*. You got past that fear for her, because her safety was more important to you than your fear."

Tears blurred my vision, and I tried to blink them away, but I couldn't keep them at bay. Emrhys wiped them away as they fell.

"You're so much stronger than you give yourself credit for. Cass was right when he said we're all so lucky to have you. I know I don't deserve you after what I put you through. I may have been following your grandfather's orders, but I knew you were different from the moment I saw you."

"Thank you," I whispered around the lump of emotion stuck in my throat.

Leaning down, he kissed each of my cheeks as if he was kissing away the tears that had fallen, and then gave me a feather-light kiss on the lips. "Now... we've got some work to do."

Chapter Four

Cassiel

"Did Maeyve ever tell you where the brothel was?" I asked Anevae as we poured over the map, hoping to narrow down its location.

"All she told me was that it was in Western Maiviraea. I don't think she ever mentioned the name of the city it was in," she said.

"The fact that we know what part of the territory it's in helps narrow things down... a little. Brothels are often only in the big cities, so I think the first place we should look would be in Dirsethik," Emrhys explained.

"That's the capital of the West, right?" Anevae asked.

"It is," I confirmed, continuing to watch her.

Anevae's gaze met mine, brows deeply furrowed. "What if she's not there? Are there a lot more big cities in Western Maiviraea?"

Emrhys stepped toward our sweet girl and rubbed soothing circles on her back. "Western Maiviraea isn't very populated overall. Most shifters try to stay as far away from Kaeuil as possible, because demons like to cause lots of problems."

"Okay. Well, how many big cities are we talking?" Anevae asked hesitantly.

"I think it kind of depends on your definition of big, really. Last time I was out there, only about five cities had a population that surpassed five hundred," Emrhys said.

Anevae's shoulders relaxed, and she let out a long breath. "Five feels like a manageable number. Hopefully she's in Dirsethik and we won't have to worry about looking any further."

"Have you guys tried to reach out to her again?" I asked.

Emrhys' gaze shifted to the floor. "Neither of us has tried to use our bond to communicate, even with each other, since that night. All three of us being connected means that Maeyve can usually hear our conversations."

"I don't want to worry her about what's happening here. She has enough to deal with on her own without adding our worries on top of it," Anevae said.

"I know you're trying to protect her, but if you guys can still communicate with her, she may be able to tell us what city she's in or give us some landmarks she may have passed on her way there," I said.

Anevae turned to look at Emrhys and bit her lip piercing, playing with it momentarily. "She was pretty insistent that she didn't want us coming after her when we spoke to her the night the madam took her. But she's got to know I can't just sit here and do nothing when I'm responsible for putting her in that situation."

"It wouldn't hurt to ask her. She can't get upset at you for wanting to get her out. I mean, look at what you were willing to do to take your sister home," Emrhys said, trying to reassure her again.

"Maeyve has always done things on her own, though. Until recently, she had no other choice. Her mom only supported her until she was old enough to work at the brothel. I just want her to know that she's not alone anymore, and she doesn't have to do everything by herself," Anevae said, eyes filling with tears again.

I wrapped my arms around her and she leaned into the embrace, holding me tight as her tears soaked my shirt. It hurt to see her so broken and upset when she talked about what Maeyve went through as a child. I hadn't heard her whole story yet, but even that bit made me furious with her mother.

When Anevae's tears slowed, I eased my hold on her and placed a gentle kiss on the top of her head. "As soon as she's back with us, we can ensure she never has to endure something so terrible again."

"I know, but I still worry," she whispered.

"It's okay to worry, sweetheart. Just don't let your fear become the center of your attention because then you won't be able to see the situation clearly," I said, looking back into her eyes. "I need you to close your eyes for a moment and take a big, deep breath. When you let it out, focus on your bond with Maeyve. Then, I want you to continue that cycle until your sole focus is on that bond. Can you do that for me?"

Looking up at me, she nodded and followed my directions, inhaling and exhaling with slow, measured breaths. When I glanced at Emrhys, who was still standing with one hand on her back, he was following the breathing exercise, too.

"Do you feel her?" I asked quietly, so I didn't interrupt her concentration. When she nodded, I asked, "What do you feel?"

"I can feel her emotions, but the way they're presenting themselves in my body is strange. Her anger feels like an intense heat in my cheeks and ears; while her fear tastes sour, making me feel like I want to throw up; but her... curiosity feels like goosebumps all over my body."

"What else do you feel from her?"

"Determination. She wants to get back to me—to us."

I was curious if Emrhys felt the same things from Maeyve as Anevae, but I didn't want to interrupt him to ask. Instead, I asked Anevae, "Can you feel how she is physically? Is she hurt?"

Anevae shook her head. "She feels fine. Maybe a little hungry, but who knows the last time she had a good meal?"

Emrhys caught me off guard when he whispered, "That's incredible."

I smiled. "Whenever you're worried about her, I want you to do this; use the bond to check on her when she can't answer you. But I also want you to reach out to her tonight, if you can. It's getting pretty close to lunch, so we need to wrap things up for now."

With a nod, she opened her eyes and got on her tiptoes to give me another kiss. Then she whispered, "Thank you, my wise little owl."

Emrhys' laugh echoed through the room, and I scowled at him. "What's so funny?"

The vampire rolled his eyes. "Do you even know what an owl *is*?"

My scowl deepened. "N-no. I just thought it was a term of endearment or something."

Anevae turned and playfully smacked Emrhys in the belly. "Would you be nice, *please*? Cassiel, an owl is a type of bird in the human realm that was believed to be related to the Greek goddess of wisdom. They also have big eyes that most people believe are 'all-seeing.' My calling you 'my wise little owl' was supposed to be sweet."

Raising an eyebrow, I said, "I guess I don't understand. Why was Emrhys laughing?"

Emrhys laughed again. "Because, Cassiel, you are far from *little*. And I thought she called you an owl because you have wings—"

Anevae landed another blow on his chest, hard enough that he let out an *oof*. "Be. Nice. Emrhys. I'm not saying please again. To clarify, I did not call Cass an owl because he has wings. I called him a *wise owl* because he's so knowledgeable!"

"I hope he knows a lot. You do realize how old he is, right?" Emrhys asked sarcastically.

"What does his age have to do with knowing a lot? He's an angel with unlimited access to the library in Baeruil, where they keep records of nearly everything," Anevae snapped.

Emrhys shook his head. "When Cass tells you exactly how old he is, you'll understand why I say I hope he knows a lot."

Anevae looked at me with an eyebrow raised, and I shot Emrhys a glare. *Damn vampire.*

"While I have unlimited access to Baeruil's library, Emrhys has a point. I've been alive for over one thousand years. I stopped counting after I reached that point."

Anevae's jaw dropped to the floor, but she recovered quickly. "One *thousand* years? Like an entire millennium? Holy shit, that's a long time."

"Exactly my point—" Emrhys began, but Anevae hit him in the gut.

"Would you stop it? I get it. He's got several hundred years on—wait. How old are you, Em?"

Emrhys stood tall and puffed out his chest. "I just turned one hundred a few weeks before you came to Caellaias."

Anevae pursed her lips. "I'm far too used to human years. One hundred just sounds so... old. One thousand still sounds impossible."

Curiosity killed the cat, and I asked, "Well, how old are you?"

She rolled her lip between her teeth, and her cheeks flared red. "I'm currently twenty-eight, nearly twenty-nine."

"You're still a babe! Barely old enough to be considered of age," Emrhys said teasingly, reaching out to pinch her cheek.

"Fuck you," Anevae hissed and batted his hand away.

Quick on his feet, he swept the hair from her shoulder and grabbed her throat lightly, pulling her against him. After placing a kiss on her neck, he said, "Is that an invitation? Because I'd love to sink my cock into your sweet cunt right now. If you're lucky, maybe Cass will join the fun."

Anevae's nostrils flared. "As fantastic as that sounds, we should focus on wrapping this stuff up like we discussed earlier."

With one more kiss on her blazing cheek, Emrhys released her and teased, "Why do you have to be right?"

When lunchtime came around, I bid Anevae and Emrhys goodbye. "I'm going to head to Baeruil for a while so I can do some work on the prophecy. I should be back by the time you guys are done with dinner. Then, we can talk about anything I may have found."

Anevae's brows furrowed as she wrapped her arms around me. "Be careful."

I huffed out a small laugh and pulled her close, kissing the top of her head. "Always, sweetheart."

After a moment, I squeezed her shoulders, letting her know it was time to go. She sighed and gave me a quick kiss before hurrying off with Emrhys. Once she was out of sight, I conveyed myself to my room inside Castle Rilvara, where I retrieved my robes, then continued to my room in Baeruil.

Just using my power had me feeling irritated, though. I felt like I failed Anevae because I couldn't convey us to Maeyve and bring her back. Conveyance only allowed me to travel somewhere I'd visited, and I hadn't ever been to any part of Maiviraea as far as I could recall. When I told Anevae this, I watched the ounce of hope she had left disintegrate, breaking my heart.

As soon as my feet hit the floor of my room in Baeruil, I burst through the door, heading straight for the library. I had to focus on something else before I let my anger get the best of me. This one situation, as painful and heart-wrenching as it was, couldn't be the reason my composure broke; I'd spent far too many years working hard on solidifying it.

When I entered the library, The Librarian appeared before me, stopping me in my tracks. "I believe this is the most I have seen you since you were young. What brings you to my library today, Cassiel?"

A smile crested my lips. "How is it you seem to know every time I'm here?"

"This is my library, is it not?"

"That doesn't mean you'd know I was here. Does anyone else get this lovely greeting every time they show up?" I teased.

"You may be a tad bit special, but do not tell anyone else," she said with a wink. "Now, are you going to tell me what brings you here today?"

With a slight chuckle, I said, "I'm still trying to figure out this prophecy. I just needed somewhere quiet and without prying eyes to work on it."

"I see. You are welcome in my library anytime. But, since you are here, may I request your help to put some tomes away in the cage?"

"Sure. I'll follow you."

Spinning on her heel, she began the trek to the cage. When we got inside, she asked in a hushed tone, "How is the girl?"

I eyed her suspiciously, not entirely sure who she was referring to yet. "She's... okay."

"Even after the king sent her mate away?"

My brows slammed down with her question, knowing she was talking about Anevae and Maeyve. "H-how do you know about that?"

Quirking one of her eyebrows, she smirked. "I have my ways."

"To answer your question, Anevae is fine, even with everything going on."

"The madam took her back for a good reason, even though it doesn't seem like it yet."

My stomach roiled. "What *good* reason could there be for a woman to be forced into sex work?"

"It is not what you think. That was not the purpose of her return to the brothel. You will find out more before long."

"How do you know about everything with Anevae and Maeyve?" I asked, irritation lacing my voice.

"That is something I cannot discuss with you at the moment. Have you deciphered anything else about the prophecy since we spoke last?"

"No. I can't find enough resources about the ancient language to translate it."

The Librarian nodded slowly. "That does make things very difficult. I do wish I could be of more assistance. Things will all begin to make sense soon enough, dear Cassiel. I must get back to the library. Have a good day."

Chapter Five

Maeyve

After a day of silence in the carriage, Madam Tanith tried to strike up a conversation with me.

"I'm so pleased to have you back, Maeyve," she said in her sickeningly sweet voice. "You know, the little stunt you pulled left your mother devastated for years. But it's safe to say she's gotten over it now."

"Good for her," I said, trying not to allow her to get under my skin.

The madam huffed out a breath. "Seems you've changed very little since you left. You're still cold as ever, even toward the woman who gave you life. How sad."

"Maybe if she hadn't abandoned me at such a young age and left me to be abused, I would care more."

The madam tsked. "Your mother knew what would happen if she gave birth to you in my brothel. However, she knew what would've happened if she hadn't, either. You've always belonged to me."

I growled, whipping my head in her direction. "I belong to no one but myself, and you cannot control me."

She raised a brow as she considered her next words. "I let you get away with too much last time. Now, you're so unruly and temperamental. Things are going to be *very* different this go around. You will do as you're told, otherwise there will be consequences."

I returned my gaze to the window. "You don't scare me anymore. Fucking bitch."

Madam Tanith's poise snapped. She launched herself at me, grabbed me by the cheeks, and forced me to look back at her. "You have no clue what I am capable of, little girl. I went easy on you because you were still so young, but I will no longer hold back. When we return, you will begin seeing a wide range of clients. Then, when I'm sure you won't try to run off again, your job seeking high-profile targets will restart. Am I making myself clear?"

My body shook with rage. Ripping my face from her grasp, I hissed, "Go fuck yourself, you disgusting waste of space. I'll kill the first person who tries to touch me without my permission and then hang their corpse above the entrance to the brothel for everyone to see."

The back of her hand cracked across my face before she got even closer. "If you lay your hands on one of my clients, I will lock you in the dungeon for an entire week without food or socialization."

My stomach dropped. The dungeon was the place of my nightmares during my childhood. It was where she'd sent the girls who'd stepped out of line, often going as far as torturing them down there. During my first time at the brothel, I did everything imaginable to stay out of there, as did many of the others.

"Do I make myself clear?" she asked again.

Nostrils flared, I nodded.

The madam straightened herself out and sat back in her seat. "Perfect. We'll be home soon."

It took us a total of two days to get to the brothel in the carriage. *Two fucking days.* Yet it took the bitch less than twelve hours to get to the castle when Amaroc called upon her. Being away from my mates had a bone-deep ache growing in my chest that only got worse as the distance between us grew.

Even my mating marks ached, but I'd have to keep them covered at all times in the brothel. I still wasn't sure if the madam knew I'd mated with not one, but two others. Anevae's mark on my neck was the one I worried most about because it would give me away easily. Emrhys' mark was much easier to cover with it being on my shoulder, so I wasn't as worried about it. The revealing clothes the madam would force me to wear concerned me, though. Covering anything while wearing them would be nearly impossible. But then I wondered if clients would even pay attention to the marks on my body when all they wanted was to get off or inflict pain.

Continuing to think about my mates made my chest heavy with sadness again. I missed them and hoped everything was okay, but I didn't dare reach out to them. If I did, I worried they would bombard me with questions I didn't have the answers to, and I didn't want to tell them what Madam Tanith had planned for me. I couldn't live with myself if they risked their lives to save me—I'd get out on my own one way or another.

When the carriage pulled outside the brothel, Madam Tanith grabbed my chin and forced my attention to her again. "Everyone will be eager to see that you're alive and well. Act happy to see them. A few newer girls have also joined over the last several years. I'm sure you'll make friends with a few of them. Other than that, I will only say this one more time: you will behave yourself. I won't hesitate to throw you in that dungeon with even one slight misstep. Got it?"

"Yes, *ma'am.*"

Finally releasing my chin, she moved to exit the carriage. "I'm glad we're on the same page. Let's keep it that way."

I clenched my jaw as I carefully climbed out behind her. To my surprise, the mansion I'd never wanted to see again was still standing separate from the city's other buildings. Even though the city had grown exponentially during my fifty-year absence, the madam managed to keep that a constant. The exterior of the massive, white-stoned building hadn't changed a bit, either. Before me, the door sported the same red as when I left, and the window furnishings were the same shade I remembered. When I was young, one of the girls told me the madam used red accents all over the mansion because it was the color of lust, making it perfect for the brothel.

Feet firmly on the ground, Madam Tanith cleared her throat, telling me I was taking too long. After a deep breath, I grabbed the skirt of my dress so I could catch up with the evil woman. But the closer I got to the brothel, the faster my heart hammered in my chest.

As I approached the door, I took deep, even breaths. I had to shut down all my emotions, especially my fear, if I had any hopes of getting out. With each step, I built up the mental walls it would take to get me through the time I was going to spend in the brothel. Then I shoved every emotion behind those walls; I couldn't let them cloud my judgment.

When I stepped through the doorway, I was a blank slate, ready for whatever was going to be thrown at me. Several girls rushed forward and wrapped me up in hugs, telling me how excited they were to see me. I patted each one with a forced smile plastered on my face.

Once they dispersed, my mom came into view, standing on the opposite side of the room, staring at me. In her arms was a sleeping toddler. What caught me off guard was the little girl huddled against my mom's side with features similar to mine, except her eyes were a vivid green. When my eyes drifted back to my mom's again, she clenched her jaw and turned to leave. The little girl beside her stood there staring at me until my mom grabbed her bicep and dragged her down the hall.

Madam Tanith strode up beside me, shooing the girls who still lingered. With a sly grin, she said, "I told you she'd gotten over you."

The only reaction I graced her with was shrugging my shoulders before I went back to looking over the common room.

With a huff, Madam Tanith summoned a girl to join us. "Sameera, Maeyve will be occupying the other bed in your room. I'm going to clear your schedule for the evening and let the hostess know you'll be unavailable for the rest of the night, so you can help Maeyve get settled back in. Someone will be up with a new wardrobe and some birth control for her before dinner is served. Maeyve, get cleaned up and make sure to get lots of rest this evening. You'll get back to seeing clients tomorrow, and I want you well-rested for it because the one you're starting with is one of my most frequent customers. I have a feeling you'll remember him."

My stomach roiled, hoping she was wrong. Her frequent fliers had been among the first to lay hands on me when I first began seeing clients all those years ago, to prepare me for anyone that could come my way. Back then, I was still a little girl and wasn't prepared for what they put me through. Because I was an adult this time, I feared what they would do to me.

I forced the fear and memories behind my mental wall and met Sameera's gaze. Her vibrant pink eyes were rimmed with dark makeup, making them seem even more intense. A wide smile spread across her pouty lips, showing off her pristine white teeth and pointy canines as she held out her well-manicured hand to shake. "I've heard a lot about you from Moranna. It's nice to actually meet you."

Hesitantly, I took her hand, but when the telltale tingles spread up my arm, it took everything in me not to jump back. My eyes shot up to Sameera's, which had widened to the size of saucers. But she maintained her composure well enough that Madam Tanith didn't notice something was off.

"It's a pleasure to meet you as well, Sameera. I just wish it was under different circumstances. Let's just say this place doesn't hold many good memories," I said as I withdrew my hand from her grasp.

"I'll leave you ladies to it, and I'll see you both at dinner this evening. Please behave, Maeyve," said the madam before heading toward the stairs.

Sameera glanced around the room and cleared her throat. "Let's get you up to our room, shall we?"

"That would be great," I said, my tone skeptical and reserved.

With quick steps, she led me to the back of the room and up the stairs, taking me to the third floor. When we were about halfway down the hall, she spun around and threw me up against the wall with her arm pressing on my throat—the sleeve of her shirt putting a much needed barrier between her skin and mine.

"What the fuck was that down there?" she hissed, loosening the pressure on my throat ever so slightly so I could talk, but couldn't pull away.

I scowled. "I think you're perfectly aware of what that was."

She clenched and unclenched her jaw a few times as she stared me down.

When it was clear she wasn't going to say anything else, I rolled my eyes. "Whatever. Can you let me go, please? I'm not going to hurt you."

After a moment, she lowered her arm and took a step back. But when I brought up my hand to massage my throat, she gasped. Then she grabbed my hand and yanked me further down the hall, presumably to our room. Once we were both through the door, she slammed it shut and shoved me onto a pristine, all-white bed.

"Let me see your neck," she demanded.

I struggled not to reach up for it right away. We needed to talk about what had happened downstairs with the tingles, but she was already on the defense. "Why?"

"Just let me see your damn neck, please."

Throwing all caution to the wind, I swept my hair away from the mating mark she'd likely seen when I rubbed my neck in the hall. Her brows slammed down as she took a step closer to inspect.

"A-are you—" she began.

"Yes. I'm mated to a woman who is half shifter, half fae." Reaching for my shoulder, I showed her Emrhys' mark. "I'm also mated to a purebred male vampire. But I was mated to the female first."

Her jaw dropped as she placed her hand on her chest and stepped back. "That's impossible."

My mouth got away from me faster than I could catch it. "She's fated to five beings across the kingdom and has connected with three of us, but she's only mated to myself and one other, thus far. We believe we've found another. However, I suspect you may be the last one."

Leaning in, she hissed, "I'm already mated to my fated mate, so that's impossible."

"You keep saying that. Do me a favor and explain the tingling when we touched earlier if we're not fated."

"How the fuck am I supposed to know what's causing the tingling?"

"Because you're adamant that we can't be fated. Do you get tingles like that when you touch your fated mate?" I asked, quirking my head. "I know I do when I touch Anevae and Emrhys."

Shaking her head vigorously, she turned to her bed. "That's impossible."

"Improbable? Yes. Impossible? No," I said, nonchalantly. Then, I asked, "Who is your mate, if you don't mind me asking?"

She considered me for a minute before responding, "Even though I don't know if I should trust you, I guess there's no harm in telling you my mate's name. You did tell me yours after all. His name is Amareon."

Shooting up in bed, I asked, "As in the high lord of Eirvanna's son?"

Her brows furrowed again. "You know him?"

I bit my lip, trying to think of the best way to explain. "I know of him. If you're mated to him, it might explain some things, though."

"We've got time for you to explain. Dinner won't be ready for a few more hours, and I doubt they'll be up with the items Madam Tanith requested anytime soon."

Sighing, I lay back again and massaged my temples. "Fine. How long have you known Amareon?"

"About ten or so years. Why?"

"How much do you know about him?"

Her bed shifted as she stood and began pacing. "I'd love to say I know everything about him, but I know that's unrealistic. We've shared a lot about our lives with each other. Again, why do you want to know?"

"My questions have a purpose, and I'm getting to it."

She huffed. "Fine."

"Thank you. During the time you knew him, did he ever enter the human realm?"

Her pacing stopped. "In the two years we spent together, no, he didn't. Once I was... captured, I'm not sure if he did or not."

I sat up, coming face to face with her, staring at me with her arms crossed. "You were captured? By whom?"

Turning away from me, she began pacing again. "I don't want to talk about it."

I rolled my eyes. "Okay. What do you know about your mate's family?"

"All I know is that his father is the lord of Eirvanna, and he *had* a twin brother."

My heart pounded with the new information. "Do you know what his twin's name was?"

"Ambrose."

My jaw dropped as everything fell into place. "She was right about him. And now I've found the missing link," I whispered, mainly to myself.

Sameera tapped her foot. "Explain."

"Give a girl a second. Damn. And would you knock that off?" I gestured to her tapping foot. "It's only going to irritate me if you continue that shit."

She let out an exasperated sigh and was about to say something when there was a knock on the door. We stood, silent, as an elderly woman walked into our room, arms full of clothing. Behind her was a younger woman with more clothes and two glass bottles.

The elderly woman stopped at the foot of my bed and gave me a wide smile. "Welcome back, Maeyve."

I didn't immediately recognize the woman, but it clicked when I heard her voice. "Greta?"

"It has been far too long, my dear."

I jumped to my feet, yanked the clothes from her arms, and threw them on the bed before wrapping her in a big hug. "I didn't recognize you. While I hate to say it, you've aged rather drastically since I last saw you."

"I have, my dear. Many beings age much faster when we near the end of our time in this realm," she said quietly.

"Aren't you only like a thousand years old?" I asked.

With a slight chuckle, she patted my back, and I released her. "I am, but my kind aren't known to live as long a life as the rest of the fae. Technically, I've already outstayed my welcome by a few hundred years."

"Well, I'll be sad to see you go when the time comes," I said, then turned to the other woman and took the items she held. "Thank you both for the clothes and medicine."

"You're welcome. We will see you at dinner, dearies," Greta said, before ushering the other woman out of the room.

Once their footsteps were out of earshot, Sameera said, "I'm still waiting for that explanation."

"By the gods, you are so impatient!" I grumbled as I plopped onto my bed again. "Have a seat. This may take a bit."

Reluctantly, she did as I suggested, and I told her everything I knew about Anevae's experience with Ambrose in the human realm, even though it wasn't my story to tell. Sameera's mood shifted when I told her about how Ambrose used to treat Anevae.

"Amareon is nothing like his brother. He's the sweetest man I've ever met," she said, trying to defend her mate.

"I'm not implying they're anything alike, but Anevae had no way of knowing he was a twin. So when she saw Amareon in the ballroom, she thought it was Ambrose and panicked. When the king introduced them, she noticed his eyes were two different colors while Ambrose's eyes were both green—"

"The lord mentioned their eyes a few times when he spoke of the twins. Apparently, that was the only way most could tell them apart, but I'd never met Ambrose in the two years I was around the family, so I can't confirm."

Shooting her a dirty look, I continued, "I wasn't done explaining everything—"

"You're a real bitch sometimes."

"And you're annoying! Would you fucking stop interrupting me? Anyway, back to what I was saying. When Amareon greeted her, he kissed her knuckles, and she felt the tingles so we think he's her mate from Eirvanna."

Sameera's jaw ticked, and then she lay down. Several moments of silence passed before I finally got up and put away my new clothes—if you could even call the strips of cloth that. When they were all arranged to my liking, I grabbed one of the glass bottles. Unscrewing the top, I pinched the dropper and withdrew it, placing three drops underneath my tongue. The stuff tasted nasty, but it would keep me from ovulating, which meant I wouldn't get pregnant if a mishap occurred. While in the human realm, I'd acquired some of the tonic just to keep my period at bay. If I didn't have to bleed for days on end and suffer through the cramps, I didn't want it.

After replacing the dropper, I grabbed the other bottle and put them both in the drawer of my nightstand for easy access. I would have to take the tonic once in the morning and once in the evening in order for it to work properly.

When I was done, I sat on the bed again and glanced at Sameera. "From your teeth, I can tell you're a shifter. Were both of your parents shifters?"

"No. My dad was a shifter, but my mom was a low-level succubus."

"That confirms it. You're her last mate."

Chapter Six

Sameera

For the remainder of the day, Maeyve's words played on repeat in my mind, '*That confirms it. You're her last mate.*' But that didn't make sense. When learning about fated mates in school, they made two things clear: there were no same-sex fated mates, and no one had more than one.

Maeyve was a walking contradiction to both of those claims, though. She'd mated with Anevae first. And then she mated with the male vampire afterward. To make matters worse, every time I touched her, it brought about the tingles I'd only ever felt from Amareon.

The constant ache in my chest intensified at the thought of Amareon. The only way I'd been able to find that could soothe that ache was by opening our bond slightly to check on him. When I opened it completely, it felt like my chest was ripping open, so I only did it when I wanted to risk speaking to him. Opening our bond was the only way we could communicate, though. When we did chance it, we couldn't stay connected for too long because the pain in my chest became crippling and I couldn't function for hours.

Dinner was a welcome and eventful distraction that evening thanks to Maeyve's return. Anytime anyone tried to ask her what she'd been doing the last fifty years, she said she wasn't interested in talking about it. Even though no one liked that answer, they eventually accepted it and carried on conversation as usual.

The only person who refused to address Maeyve was her mother. Moranna kept her distance and made sure both of her children stayed with her throughout dinner. Maeyve glared in her mother's direction for the entire evening, tears welling every now and then, but she sat as far away from Moranna as possible. They couldn't keep their eyes off each other for long, though.

It made me sad to see Maeyve and her mother keeping such distance from each other when they'd been apart for so long. When I first got to the brothel, Moranna had told me so much about her daughter. She loved Maeyve and even compared me to her several times. I looked up to them both, even going as far as to say I viewed Moranna as a mother figure and mentor. But seeing the way she acted at dinner with her daughter alive and well had questions flying through my mind.

When Maeyve finished her food, she excused herself and shuffled out of the room, drawing my attention back to her. I ate the last of my dinner quickly so I could join her and make sure she was okay. She'd reached the second floor before I finally caught up to her.

She didn't even turn around before she spoke to me. "Before you even ask, I'm fine. I just need to get some sleep. You heard the madam about my day tomorrow."

"How did you know it was me?" I asked, genuinely curious.

Maeyve's eyes darted around. "Not here. Anyone could hear us. I'm going to our room. You're welcome to join me or go back to dinner."

"Fine. Lead the way."

Once our door was closed, I asked my question again, "How did you know it was me when I came up behind you?"

"My body recognizes yours now that we've made skin-to-skin contact."

Raising an eyebrow, I said, "I don't remember that happening with Amareon so I feel like you just made that up."

She scoffed. "You've been away from your mate for a while; I've been in contact with mine a hell of a lot more recently."

"I still don't know if I believe that we're fated."

She whirled around to face me. "Touch my hand or any part of my bare skin again. If that's what it takes for you to believe this is real, by all means, do it. The sooner you come to terms with this, the sooner we can return to our mates."

I crossed my arms and furrowed my brows. "Why are you being such a bitch?"

Maeyve scoffed, "I don't want to fucking be here, and I would do anything to be with my mates. Something I *thought* you would understand being separated from Amareon."

"I do, but this is a lot to take in, and I can't wrap my head around everything you've told me."

"It still doesn't make complete sense to me and my mates either, but we're embracing it—*living* it. Hopefully, when we reunite with our mates, they'll know more about the prophecy."

"Wait a damn minute. Prophecy? You never mentioned a *prophecy*. What does it say?" I asked as I approached

Maeyve groaned and threw herself on her bed. "The only thing we know right now is that it speaks of a woman who would have a mate from each of the territories, and they would help her unite the kingdom somehow."

"So you're saying that Anevae is this woman?"

"Basically, that's what we've come to understand, yes."

"Basically? This is too big of a deal to have an answer like *basically*," I whisper-yelled.

Maeyve sighed as she reached to cover her eyes. "We don't know everything yet. Cassiel, Anevae's angel mate, has been working on trying to figure out the prophecy, but it hasn't exactly been easy. We've only been working on this for a few weeks max."

Grinding my teeth, I paced between our beds. It seemed the best course of action would be to reach out to Amareon so we could discuss what had happened since Maeyve came to the brothel. He could gather more information from the others at the castle—answer some of my pressing questions—and put my mind at ease.

In turn, I'd have to suffer through the pain it took to make that connection.

When Maeyve and I got into bed that night, I prepared myself for the pain that would come when I reached out to Amareon. Maeyve sharing a room with me complicated things. I had to remain as quiet as possible so I didn't wake her.

Closing my eyes, I focused on the bond with Amareon, enjoying the warmth it provided me, before reaching out to him, *Baby?*

Mere moments passed before his panicked, deep voice echoed in my mind, *Kitten? Is everything okay?*

Pain seared through my chest, and I smacked my hand over my mouth to quiet the involuntary whimper it caused.

Amareon's sorrow passed through our bond. *I'm so sorry, kitten. I know it hurts. Take your time.*

I was so busy breathing through the pain, I didn't hear Maeyve get up from her bed and approach mine. "Sameera, what happened? Is everything okay?"

Clenching my teeth, I hissed, "I'm fine. Go back to your bed."

She leaned over me and grasped my shoulder, trying to get me to face her while still respecting my unspoken boundaries. But I refused to move. I didn't want her to see me in that state.

"Sameera. Look at me," she demanded, still clinging to me.

Fuck. Baby, I'll be right back. My new roomie won't leave me alone, I said to Amareon.

I'll be waiting.

When I didn't answer fast enough for her, Maeyve shifted her hand to my bare arm. Tingles shot through my body, and the pain in my chest fizzled, but my anger boiled over. Flinging myself off the bed, I shoved her onto her own, where she landed flat on her back, her neon orange eyes wide.

"I was *trying* to talk to my mate when you so rudely interrupted me."

"You were in pain doing so. Why?" she asked.

I let out a long sigh and threw my head back. "I don't have time for this right now! Can we please talk about this after I'm done?"

Maeyve's brows dropped, sadness etched across her face. "I'm sorry. I heard you whimper and kind of panicked."

Rolling my eyes, I said, "I'm fine. Thanks for checking at least." Then, I realized something. "My chest doesn't hurt anymore. When you touched my arm, it was like the tingling feeling made it go away."

"That doesn't surprise me. Like I said earlier, our bodies recognize each other."

"This is all so fucking weird," I said, glancing down at the floor. "Thank you for helping with the pain. If you don't mind, I'd like to talk to my mate by myself, please."

"You're welcome. Wake me up if you need anything," she said before crawling back under her covers.

I followed suit and closed my eyes, reaching back out to Amareon.

What's going on, kitten? he asked when he felt the bond fully open back up.

I don't really know how to explain it without sounding crazy.

His laugh resounded through our bond, sending chills through my body. It'd been far too long since I'd heard it in person. *What's going on? You know I'll never think you're crazy.*

Do you know of a woman named Anevae? I asked cautiously.

I do. She's the king's granddaughter. I met her a couple of days ago. He was throwing a ball to celebrate the return of Princess Cordilaen and the arrival of her daughters. My father insisted I accompany him.

When you met her, was there anything... unusual that happened?

Amareon paused for a moment. *Yes, there was. I'm trying to figure it out, but I haven't been able to speak with her about it yet.*

What happened?

D-do you remember what it felt like when we first touched?

Of course I do. I'll never forget it.

He hesitated before continuing, *That happened with her, too. I know it should be impossible...*

I-I had something similar happen to me today.

There was tension in his voice when he asked, *Was it with a client?*

No, baby. It was with another courtesan—a woman. You might've heard of her or even seen her at the ball.

A woman? Are you sure you felt the same tingling sensation with her as you did with me?

I promise, it was the same thing.

Amareon sighed. *Fine. Who is she?*

Her name is Maeyve. She claims she's Anevae's mate, too.

His shock rushed through our bond, nearly knocking the breath out of me. *The king pointed out a 'mutt' when Lord Amaroc showed up, followed by a madam who escorted the woman out. Anevae was distraught when it happened, and now it makes sense why. Does Maeyve have mixed blood?*

She does. Her father was an incubus that never became a part of her life, and her mother is Moranna.

Have you tried to speak to Maeyve about what happened?

Yes.

Aaaand? He said, drawing the word out. *What did she say?*

I fiddled with my thumbs while contemplating how to tell him what Maeyve had told me. I started by explaining to him the little I knew about the prophecy. *I don't have the whole story, and I need you to ask the angel Cassiel about it. She claims we're the missing pieces to this prophecy.*

His shock hit me harder, almost suffocating me. After several moments of silence, he said, *With what happened between Anevae and me, plus between you and Maeyve, it makes sense; I guess. I still just don't know how to feel about it. We never had time to solidify our bond, and now I'm supposed to be sharing you with others? I haven't seen you—held you—in close to eight years and I miss you so fucking much.*

Tears streaked down my face before I could stop them. *I miss you so much. There's not a day that goes by that I don't wish I could be with you. I'm working on finding a way out. Maybe Maeyve coming here was the exact thing I needed. Plus, Anevae and the others will do everything they can to get her out, and she'll insist that I come with. So you might see me sooner than you think.*

I'm sorry, kitten. I'm sorry I haven't been able to get you out sooner. What my father did was wrong, and I'll make sure that he and the others responsible for putting you in there get what they deserve.

I know. One day it'll happen. I love you, baby.

A tinge of sadness slipped through our bond, even though I knew he was trying to hold it back. *I love you, too. Get some sleep. I have some things to take care of early in the morning, so I need to rest. We'll speak soon.*

Moments later, our bond slipped closed, and the ache in my chest returned. The sudden onset had me hissing through my teeth. I rolled onto my side as tears filled my eyes, both from the pain and emptiness in my chest. Behind me, the bed dipped, and a comforting pair of arms wrapped around me—Maeyve.

"What's hurting you so much?" Maeyve asked as she placed her hand on the exposed part of my chest.

The ache eased again and I was able to take in a deep breath. "Every time I activate my bond with Amareon, I get an awful pain in my chest that gets worse the longer I have the bond open. I'm not aware of it happening for Amareon, but he's been very understanding with it and always gives me the time I need to adjust to the pain."

"I'm so sorry, but you'll see him soon enough. I *will* get us out of here one way or another."

I leaned into her and shook my head. "You don't understand. If I leave, he'll only come looking for me again."

"Who?" she asked, concern lacing her voice.

"A demon named Cahir. He's my 'grandmother's' general."

"Why would he come after you? Were you running from your grandmother?"

"I was. Until my 'grandmother' sold me to Madam Tanith." When Maeyve's brows furrowed, I closed my eyes and took a deep breath. "She's not my biological grandmother. My mom, Shivani, grew up in the slums of Tyrkenea with my biological grandmother, Akantha, who was a succubus working as a prostitute. Akantha had never been married and never brought home a man, so my mom never knew who her father was. That changed when my mom came of age. Akantha told her that her father was the Lord of Kaeuil, but begged my mom not to approach him. Of course, my mom didn't listen.

"Eventually, my mom went to see the lord, my grandfather, and when she did, she was shocked. They shared so many facial features that it was like looking in a mirror. The most striking similarity was their eyes. Akantha had green eyes, but my mom's eyes were pink, just like the lord's.

"My mom confronted the lord in the town square which quickly gained the attention of the others around them, so he dismissed her and called her crazy. Later that night, he showed up at Akantha's house, asking to speak with my mother, and after a long conversation, he admitted that she was in fact his daughter.

"When she tried to ask questions, he refused to answer them and told her that she needed to leave the territory and never come back. Initially she refused. She had never been away from home, and didn't want to leave Akantha behind. Then he told her that if word got back to his wife, the lady of Kaeuil, she would kill my family.

"He offered to pay her way and give her money to settle herself somewhere far away from Tyrkenea. She accepted, and the next day, she left for Maiviraea. She traveled for a little while, exploring the land and looking for the best place to settle down, and that's when she met my dad. He was a lynx shifter doing business here in Western Maiviraea. He asked her to travel back to Eastern Maiviraea with her, and she agreed because she was already falling in love with him. A few years later, they got married, and a few years after that, I was born.

"When I came of age, my mom started acting strange, claiming people were watching her. My dad and I thought she was just being paranoid, and we were initially dismissive of it, but it continued for months. Finally it reached a boiling point, and my dad sat her down and demanded she tell him what was going on. Eventually she broke down and told us all about who my grandfather was. We started taking her concerns seriously, constantly looking over our shoulders, always on edge, and hypervigilant about everything... but it wasn't enough," I finished on a sob, covering my mouth before I woke anyone with my cries.

Maeyve stroked my cheek, bringing me back to the moment. Her calming warmth spread through my body, and I leaned into it.

"We don't have to continue if you're not comfortable, but I would like to know what happened to your parents."

I took a deep breath and nodded. "Cahir killed them. He showed up at our house one day, claiming my grandfather sent him to check on her. My mom thought he was being genuine, so she let him in—it was a big mistake. Once the door shut behind them, he attacked her. My dad was a few towns over for a business deal when she contacted him through their mate bond. My dad tried to respond, but she was gone. He rushed home, hoping she was still alive, just unconscious. But he knew deep down she was gone; he couldn't feel her anymore.

"When my dad got home, he found her on the floor in the middle of our living room, dead. She'd been left naked and mutilated in a pool of her own blood. Her body was littered with bite marks, her neck broken, and she'd been sexually assaulted. Of course, my dad was distraught—our neighbors heard him screaming and crying for miles around the house. Then, as he cradled my mom's limp form, Cahir slit my dad's throat, nearly to the point of decapitation."

Tears streaked down my face as I looked at Maeyve. Her glossy eyes bore into mine as another pulse of warmth spread through my body.

"I'm so sorry," she whispered.

"I was on the run from the time I found them until I met Amareon. I had a couple of good years with him before Cahir finally caught up to me. He took me to my 'grandmother' and she sold me to Madam Tanith for no reason other than she could."

Maeyve leaned up to kiss my forehead. "When we leave this place, you *will* get your revenge."

Chapter Seven

Amareon

Speaking to Sameera through our bond for the first time in months was like a breath of fresh air. I missed her more than I could explain, and even that small amount of contact satiated my constant need for her a little. Without her, I felt like a piece of me was missing.

I wasn't expecting her to ask about Anevae, and I'd been hesitant to tell her about my encounter with the fae princess. Everything with her made me feel like I was going insane, and telling someone else made it sound even more crazy. I couldn't keep it a secret though. Sameera and I promised to never keep things from each other.

I'd been skeptical, but as my mate told me everything happening between her and Maeyve, things slowly pieced together. When the king introduced me to Anevae and our hands connected, something changed. Guilt washed over me because it felt like I'd found a new piece of myself I didn't know I needed while Sameera was still stuck in the brothel. I was shocked to say the least when I felt those tingles—who wouldn't have been when they'd already found their fated mate—and I was dying for answers.

The entire night after my encounter with Anevae, I tried to think of logical reasons why I felt the tingling from her. I thought maybe I was just imagining things because I couldn't come up with anything besides the fact that Anevae and I were somehow fated to each other.

My father and I had been invited to dinner with the king and his family the day after my conversation with Sameera. While there, I had to figure out a way to speak with Anevae privately, and how to have a talk with Cassiel about the prophecy.

First, though, I had to keep my composure during the carriage ride from our home in Feraetheam to the castle. It would prove to be a challenge riding that far with just my father. I'd never been his favorite—that was Ambrose's title, but my twin royally fucked up in the human realm and ended up dead. So that left my father with me, his disappointment of a son.

My mating with Sameera only further disappointed him. He knew what she was, and he was *not* impressed. Even though we were fated to each other, it did nothing to quell his anger. He could barely stand to be in the same room with her after our mating, and he avoided her at all costs. She tried to be polite—more than she should've been in my opinion—but his disgust was evident. The night Cahir took her, I knew my father had something to do with it.

His voice boomed through my bedroom, pulling me from my thoughts. "Why are you not ready yet? The carriage will be here to take us to the castle any minute."

I rose from my seat and bowed my head. "I apologize, Father. I just need to change, and I shall be ready to go."

"Get moving then. We cannot be late for this dinner with the king. The future of this family rests upon you," my father said before storming off.

Ten minutes later, I entered the living room, and my father rose from the couch. Looking me up and down, he let out a sigh. "Good enough. Don't dally. The carriage has just arrived."

"After you, Father." I gestured toward the door for him to exit.

Turning on his heel, he led me outside to the waiting carriage. We climbed in and sat opposite each other. I diverted my gaze out the window once I was settled, but I could feel my father's gaze linger on me.

On several occasions after Ambrose's passing, my father told me that when my brown eye was obscured—as it was currently—he imagined I was my twin. I made the mistake of reminding him that Ambrose was dead the first time he'd said it to me, and I was punished relentlessly.

It wasn't that I didn't miss my twin, but we were nothing alike from the moment we were born. Even though we looked identical, minus my mismatched eyes, our personalities were complete opposites. He'd always barreled into every situation without thinking anything through; I was methodical about my approach to any situation, no matter how big or small. My brother was also a narcissist. It was something he'd inherited from our father. I'd ended up being more like our mother, who seemed to do everything she could to care for and please others. In the end, that led her to leave us, though.

My parents agreed early in their marriage that my mom would stay home, take care of the home, and raise their children. My father made more than enough to support us, and he wanted to come home to a clean house and a homemade dinner every night. My mother was happy to oblige.

But then Ambrose and I were born.

Taking care of twins, who needed a lot of interaction and care, on top of constantly cooking and cleaning, made her miserable. Being the woman she was, she pushed through, but it took its toll on her. When my brother and I reached our toddler years, things almost became too much for her. Our father was too self-absorbed to notice and still expected her to care for the house without help from anyone else. This went on for years without my mother saying a thing, and I watched the joy drain from her more and more with each passing year.

Toward the end of primary school, my brother excelled at sports and played as much as he could. I was never as strong or agile as he was, and I focused more on my academics. So, while Ambrose stayed after school to play every sport imaginable with our classmates, I went home alone to join our mom. My father was rarely home before sunset, so it was always just my mom and me for a few hours. Even though Ambrose and I were more self-sufficient, and life had started to settle, her joy still hadn't made any attempt to return. I brushed it off, as everyone else had, and thought things would get better.

Nearly halfway through my last year of primary school, I came home to an eerily quiet house. My mom was almost always bustling around, cleaning or organizing, so I knew something was wrong. I called out for her as I placed my school bag on the rack near the door. When she didn't answer, a sense of dread filled me. Walking through the house, I looked inside every room and listened for any sign of her. When I reached the den, I found her. She'd hung herself from one of the wooden beams that supported the ceiling. Even though I was still such a small child, I ran to her, screaming, and tried to get her down for what felt like hours. Finally, my brother got home and helped me. But it was too late; her body was already cold and rigid.

My father showed no emotion as he sent for her to be prepared for burial. The next day, he hired our maids, Ilaria and Miray, and he quickly took a liking to them. They were willing to do anything to gain the favor of the Lord of Eirvanna, and it made me sick to watch him with them.

After my mother's burial, my father acted as if she'd been a mere inconvenience. From that point forward, I made it my mission never to let my life become like hers, devoid of joy and happiness in any form. While Ambrose was alive, I succeeded because I could avoid my father. But then it was just us two, and his sole focus became about preparing me to take over for him when he passed. He'd spent the first two decades of my life focusing on my brother, so he ended up working double time and added massive amounts of pressure to get me caught up. My mating to Sameera interfered with that big time.

When my father discovered the Lady of Kaeuil was looking for her, he turned Sameera over without hesitation, effectively taking control of my life again.

Pulling myself from my thoughts, I looked back at my father, who was still staring at me. When we made eye contact, he averted his gaze.

"I expect you to be on your best behavior, Amareon. This is an intimate dinner with the king and his family. We will discuss some very important matters this evening, and I need you to make sure you are *paying attention* when the king speaks to us. Do I make myself clear?"

With a nod and very little emotion, I said, "Yes, Father."

The rest of the carriage ride was silent. I thanked the gods because long carriage rides typically meant we spoke business or about the event we were set to attend. I wasn't worried about a small dinner with the king's family. But maybe I should've been.

When we pulled through the castle gates, the sun had just begun to set. The sky was turning into a beautiful baby pink that reminded me of Sameera's eyes. Even though it'd been years since I'd seen her, those mesmerizing eyes haunted me every time I closed mine.

The carriage stopped, and I took a moment to fix my posture before the door opened. My father exited first, and I followed as a guard escorted us to one of the sitting rooms.

At the door, the guard, a large shifter, bowed and said, "The king will be with you shortly. His staff is preparing the dining hall as we speak, and dinner will begin in about half an hour." Then he saw himself out.

My father proceeded to one couch, and I sat across from him on another. We were only there for a few minutes before the doors swung open and the king entered the room. My father and I sprung to our feet and bowed.

"Your Majesty, thank you for the invitation to join you this evening," my father said.

The king waved us off as he strolled to a liquor cabinet in the corner and poured himself a drink before sitting in a chair near the fireplace. "You are both welcome to pour yourselves a drink if interested."

My father bowed. "Thank you, Your Majesty." Then he wandered to the liquor cabinet, taking the king up on his offer.

I bowed and said, "Thank you, Your Majesty, but I will pass for now. I appreciate the invitation to attend dinner with your family tonight."

The king considered me momentarily, but then my father passed in front of him to get to his seat, and the king looked away from me. His gaze made me feel uneasy, like he was trying to see into the deepest parts of my soul.

"Amareon holds himself differently than Ambrose did. They are not much alike, are they?" The king asked my father.

After taking a sip of his drink, my father glared at me. "They may have looked identical—minus the eyes—but my boys have always had very different temperaments. Amareon has always been soft-spoken and gentle. I've been working on him, though... toughening him up and preparing him for his future."

The king drained the remainder of his glass and leaned forward to place it on the table. With his elbows on his knees, he looked me up and down again, sending shivers down my body. "Is his magic similar to his brother's?"

"It is... comparable. I have not been able to push him to the full extent of his powers in such a short amount of time," my father said, glaring at me again.

I fought the urge to roll my eyes, and the king noticed. With a light chuckle, he said, "I would love for him to stay at the castle for a while and work with the instructor I hired to assist Anevae. Cassiel successfully awakened her magic after the suppressants Cordilaen had given her wore off."

My ears perked at the mention of Anevae and Cassiel. The king's invitation would allow me to speak with them alone and together. It would also mean getting more answers because I wouldn't have to travel back and forth from the castle and my home several times.

Stroking his short beard, my father said, "I wouldn't want to intrude or have my son cause problems for you, Your Majesty. It would be a great opportunity for him, though."

The king waved my father off. "Nonsense, Koen. I have known you most of my life! If there is one thing I know, it is that you are all about order. I am certain you have instilled this in your son as well." My father nodded, and the king looked at me again, a sly grin tugging at the corner of his lips. "Then it is settled. Amareon, I will have Azur show you to a guest room when dinner ends."

Heart racing, I bowed my head slightly. "Thank you, Your Majesty. I appreciate your generosity."

As my father and the king conversed amongst themselves, I zoned out a little, thinking about what I would say to Anevae when I finally saw her. After several minutes, I shifted in my chair, wishing we'd be summoned for dinner sooner rather than later. My anxiety was getting the better of me, and I felt as though bugs were crawling under my skin. At that point, I regretted not grabbing something to drink. Fidgeting with a glass in my hands would've been far better than squirming in my chair and drawing attention to myself.

By the grace of the gods, a guard came to the door just as I was about to readjust for what felt like the millionth time. "Your Majesty, sirs, they are ready for you in the dining hall."

Chapter Eight

Anevae

When dinnertime rolled around, Emrhys escorted me to the dining hall as usual. The entire walk, and even as I entered the hall, I contemplated returning to my room, no matter the consequences. Amareon occupied the seat beside mine, where Maeyve had sat before my grandfather sent her away.

Not only had I not expected to see him at dinner, but my heart stuttered the moment I saw him. The similarities to Ambrose still struck fear in my heart. But if I looked close enough at the man before me, I was able to pinpoint the slight differences between him and the man who plagued my nightmares for so long. Amareon wasn't as muscular as Ambrose, and his skin wasn't as scarred. Where Ambrose carried himself as though he was better than everyone else, Amareon was poised and mindful of those around him.

Is everything okay? Emrhys asked through our bond.

I cleared my throat and rolled back my shoulders before continuing to my seat. *I'm fine. Seeing Amareon is very... jarring. I have to remind myself that it's not the same person who hurt me all those years ago.*

I'm sorry, baby. You shouldn't have been subjected to that.

It is what it is. It's in the past and there's nothing I can do about it now, I said as I strolled past him.

His irritation flooded through the bond, and I bit back a smile. I appreciated that he was so protective.

When I reached my seat, my grandfather met me there, pulling me into a hug. As much as I hated him touching me, I suffered through the hug. After a moment, he held me at arm's length and said, "Thank you, dear granddaughter. Please take your seat. We are just waiting on Eirian, and then we will get started with dinner."

With a slight curtsy, I took my seat as instructed. Several minutes passed, and Eiri still hadn't shown. The tick in my grandfather's jaw worsened the longer we waited, despising the tardiness his granddaughter was displaying. After ten unnerving minutes, the door flew open and my sister hurried in. Her face was beet red, and her clothing disheveled. Aeros trailed closely behind her, not looking much better.

Eiri rushed to her seat and curtsied deeply. "I am so sorry, Grandfather. I accidentally fell asleep after lessons and—"

The king rose from his seat and approached her. He pulled her into a quick embrace and whispered something I couldn't hear against her hair.

Grandfather released Eiri, and her eyes, filled with barely contained tears, connected with mine. For a brief moment, my heart broke for her, but then I reminded myself she was fully aware of what would happen if she disobeyed our grandfather's orders, and she was the reason we were here in the first place.

After everyone was seated, my grandfather clapped his hands, and dinner was served. I remained quiet throughout, as did everyone but Amareon's father. He sat directly across from me to the king's left, chatting with him nonstop. Their conversation gave my grandfather something to do besides trying to engage with those of us who wanted nothing to do with him, and I was grateful.

Beside Lord Koen, my mom sat ramrod straight with her gaze on the table. To those who didn't know her, she seemed as though she were being demure and respectful, but her posture was reserved and uncomfortable. Behind her, my father stood against the wall with his hands clasped and eyes trained on the floor. Somehow, he was still beaten and bruised despite his ability to heal quickly.

As dinner progressed, Emrhys' irritation grew and surged through our bond. I tried to keep my breathing even, but my heart rate increased with each pulse.

After the third course was served, I focused on my bond with Emrhys, hoping my message would go only to him. *I really need you to chill the fuck out. I'm feeling every single one of your emotions, and if they reach Maeyve, she'll worry. Not to mention, my heart is about to beat out of my chest. I would like not to have a panic attack in the middle of dinner.*

As if he flipped some sort of switch, Emrhys' emotions stopped coming through the bond, and my pulse slowed to a manageable pace. *I'm sorry. I've been listening to your grandfather and Lord Koen's conversation, and I don't like anything they've said.*

My pulse quickened again as my stomach sank. In my short time at the castle, I'd attended too many dinners with my grandfather that didn't end well for me, and I worried this would be another. *I wasn't listening. What have they been talking about?*

A lot of it has been about what's happening throughout Eirvanna, and how they want to handle it, but the king has mentioned purifying his bloodline several times, too.

I tried to keep my emotions in check as I asked, *How does he propose purifying his bloodline?*

Out of the corner of my eye, I saw Emrhys shift in his chair. His hesitation made me anxious, but I waited for him to speak. *I think he's arranged a marriage.*

My heart came to a standstill, and I stopped breathing for a moment. My mom's eyes snapped to mine, brows furrowed and lips pursed. I gave her the slightest shake of my head, but she just continued to look at me, so I tried again, this time tensing my jaw to prove my point. Finally, she took a deep breath and returned her attention to her plate.

When everyone was done eating, our plates were cleared by the servants. My grandfather sat back in his chair and smiled. "Let us all make our way to the sitting room."

It took everything in me not to dart in the opposite direction when we left the dining hall. But that would've greatly displeased my grandfather, and the punishment wouldn't have been worth it. At least that's what I kept telling myself.

Instead of going to the sitting room we usually went to, the guards led us to one about twice the size. It had more seating to account for the extra people who hadn't attended the prior "discussions" my grandfather subjected us to. Upon entering, my grandfather chose an armchair that looked identical to the one he preferred in the other room. Several couches were arranged in a circular pattern, focusing mainly on the king's chair and the fireplace behind him.

Being that he was the king's guest, it was customary for Lord Koen to sit to my grandfather's left, just as he'd done at the table. My mom sat next to the lord, looking as uncomfortable as ever, and my dad stood behind the couch, eyes still trained on the floor.

Emrhys directed me to the couch on my grandfather's right, where Amareon was already seated. Seeing as he was another guest, he sat closest to the king. Reluctantly, I sat beside him, trying to leave as much space between us as possible. Emrhys sat beside me as always, but kept his hands to himself and put space between us even though I'd wished he didn't. I desperately wanted his comfort at that moment.

That left Eiri and Aeros with the couch directly across from our grandfather. She wasn't happy that she was so far from him, but every time the king looked at her, she plastered a smile on her face.

Once everyone was seated, the king snapped his fingers, summoning a servant. "Would anyone else like a drink?"

Aside from my father, most of the men in the room politely accepted. My mom, sister, and I declined and sat quietly as the servant passed out drinks to the others.

My grandfather took a sip from his glass before smiling at Lord Koen and raising his glass slightly. "Koen and I have known each other for centuries, nearly our entire lives. Our families have always been very close, but we knew they would be intertwined one day." After taking another sip of his drink, his demeanor changed, and his severe gaze turned to my mom.

"I'm sorry, Father," she whimpered, keeping her gaze on the floor.

Through gritted teeth, my grandfather hissed, "Look at me when I am speaking, Cordilaen."

My mom's head lifted slowly, silver eyes bloodshot, and met his gaze. "Yes, Father."

"I am lucky that Lord Koen is such a good friend. When I announced your sister's engagement to him, she embarrassed me by running off with her demon. But I expected something like that from her, and Koen brushed it off. I did *not* expect that from you. You were my pride and joy, after all. After you fled, I spent decades fixing my reputation and allowed Koen to marry the woman of his choice, promising to fix this later down the road."

A tear rolled down my mom's cheek as she whispered, "I-I'm sorry, Father."

He waved her off as he took another drink. Then, his attention turned to Amareon and me. "When I finally found you in the human realm and I saw the girls for the first time, especially our dear Anevae, an idea dawned on me. Koen and his wife's twins, Ambrose and Amareon, were nearing the age of maturity, which meant we had another chance to combine our families. I believe Anevae was in high school when my first plan went into action. Right, Roarc?"

Everyone's attention turned to my father, who hadn't moved an inch since we entered the room. When he didn't answer, the king asked his question again, and my father said, "Yes, Your Majesty."

My mom flew to her feet and stomped around the couch to where my father stood. She shoved at his chest and screamed, "How could you!"

My father didn't move. "I had no choice, Laeney."

"There is *always* a choice, Roarc. Why didn't you tell me? We could have moved. Gone somewhere else."

Confusion swirled in my mind until everything clicked. I rose off the couch so fast Emrhys couldn't catch me until I was halfway to my grandfather. "You planted Ambrose in my high school. I have *you* to blame for the trauma he put me through, the pain he inflicted, both physically and emotionally."

"Anevae, sit back down. Now," my grandfather said, composure barely in place.

Princess, please do as he says. I know you're upset—and you have every right to be—but you cannot win this battle right now, Emrhys said through our bond.

Heaving a sigh, I glared at my father and returned to my seat, muttering, "Go fuck yourself."

My grandfather took the last sip of his drink, either choosing to ignore me or not hearing my comment, and set his glass on the end table next to his chair. "As we all know, things did not go according to plan, and Roarc killed Ambrose for his misdeeds with my granddaughter. If I had known what was happening, I would have taken matters into my own hands, but I digress. It is in the past, and I will not let the past affect the future. We have one more opportunity to intertwine our families properly."

Amareon's face was awash of all color as he looked between the king and his father. Was he kept in the dark about this plan, too?

"What do you mean by 'properly intertwine our families?'" I asked.

"Interesting that you may ask this. Koen wants what is best for this realm. He knows that one day I will die and the kingdom's fate will be passed down to my heir. This heir *must* have the royal powers to rule. I was an exception because of my position and because I had living heirs. Your mother has these powers, but is not mated to another fae. When I have her bond broken, we can rectify this, but she's also been tainted, and I do not want her on my throne.

"My only other option is you girls. After the failed attempt to get you here with Ambrose, I knew I had to get you both to Caellaias to make my decision. Getting Eirian here was easy; she is always eager to please. You, on the other hand, were my challenge. I had to figure out how to get you away from your parents. When Eirian told me about your line of work and your interests, I had the owners of Vision for the Future compelled to offer you a job. Then I went on the hunt for the perfect home for you. I am still surprised the mutt evaded my senses when I scanned the area initially. It ended up working in our favor either way."

My grandfather paused, and I clenched my jaw. "It seems my entire family isn't who I thought they were. You've all betrayed me. Eiri, you were my best friend and now I can't trust you for shit. Since we're on the topic, why don't you tell me what else you've done? I know you came to Caellaias of your own volition, but what else is there?"

Eiri shifted uncomfortably when I brought her into the conversation. "I, uh, I helped take down the ward around your house so Emrhys could get closer to you. I was trying to get you to come here without involving him first, but we needed that ward down."

My brows furrowed, and I looked to Emrhys for confirmation. He nodded, and my stomach sank. "Is that all?"

Sniffling, she nodded. I was glad to hear that there wasn't anything more, but everything she'd done was already enough. "If Eirian was so easy to get here and under your control, what did you need me for?"

"Selfishly, I have always wanted my whole family here, but since you are the eldest and do not have a brother, you are first in line for the throne," my grandfather explained.

A hollow laugh left me. "Well, I have some good news for you. I don't want your fucking throne. Honestly, I want to be anywhere but here. Give it to Eirian."

The king tsked. "There is a problem with that, though. Your sister does not possess the royal magic. We have tried several tactics to bring this magic to the surface, but none have worked. You are my only remaining heir."

Chapter Nine

Emrhys

Anevae's rage exploded through our bond, knocking the air from my lungs. I fought every instinct ingrained in me to reach out and comfort her, but I couldn't in front of the king. Instead, I pushed calming energy and words of encouragement through our bond.

A Cheshire grin spread across the king's lips as he watched Anevae's reaction. I had to admit she was doing a damn good job of keeping her magic in check with her increased emotions. But it was clear the king took great pleasure in pushing her buttons since he'd sent Maeyve away. He knew she'd let him get away with a lot more because she didn't want to upset him further.

Anevae shifted in her seat, and the king's smile fell. "Do not dare try to run off again. I have had enough of that childish behavior."

That was all it took for her to lose it. "I will not let you dictate my life! I am not your puppet to do with as you please. I refuse to marry a man who is nearly identical to the one who hurt me and nearly killed me when he was supposed to protect me. Ambrose kept me from my family and friends, basically separating me from the world during our time together. That will never, *ever* happen to me again!" Anevae yelled, lightning beginning to crackle along her arms.

Beside her, Amareon tensed. I wondered if he was aware of what his brother had done to Anevae that led to his untimely demise at the hands of her father. With his reaction, I highly doubted he'd been told about it.

The king did not take kindly to Anevae's outburst, though. "Enough! I will not have you disrespecting me in front of our guests, especially these two. They will become part of our family very soon, as your wedding will be held in a fortnight. I would like you to get acquainted in the meantime." Then, after taking a deep breath, the king said, "Amareon, Azur will show you to your suite. It is just across the hall from Emrhys', so he can help you with anything you may need."

From the darkened corner of the room, Azur appeared. He scurried to where the king sat, bowing deeply before approaching Amareon. "Good evening, sir. I would be honored to escort you to your quarters. If you will follow me, please."

Amareon rose from his seat, bowed to the king, and said, "Thank you for your hospitality, Your Majesty. Good evening, Your Highnesses. Father, I shall see you soon." Then he followed Azur out of the room.

The king sat back in his chair and crossed his legs again. "Koen, thank you for joining us for dinner. I apologize for my granddaughter's lack of respect this evening. Are you sure you do not want to stay at the castle for the evening? It is a long ride back to Feraetheam, and it is getting late."

Lord Koen waved the king off. "I have made the ride many times, Your Majesty. I am not concerned. Please let me know if my son steps out of line or causes problems before the wedding."

The king smiled and nodded. "Of course, Koen. If you hope to arrive home at a decent time, I suggest you leave soon. Not that I do not enjoy your company, but I do not want you to run into any issues along the way."

"Thank you, Your Majesty. I guess I shall be off, then." Turning his attention to Princess Cordilaen, he scooped up her hand and placed a gentle kiss on her knuckles. "Until next time, darling. It was lovely to see you again, and I enjoyed meeting your daughters." Gesturing toward Anevae, he said, "This one seems quite feisty. My son won't know what he is up against—much like how I felt before you ran away."

"I-it was nice to see you as well, Lord Koen. I hope you have safe travels home," the princess whispered, pulling her hand from the lord's grasp.

A tense silence fell over the room after that. Once the king was sure Lord Koen was far enough away from the sitting room, he focused directly on Anevae. "This is an essential union. You will not mess anything up if you value having any semblance of freedom. Do yourself a favor and get to know Amareon. You'll be pleased to find he is not like his brother."

Anevae scoffed and folded her arms across her chest. "May I be excused? *Please.*"

"I need you to understand the importance of this, Anevae," King Casimir growled.

"I understand the importance to *you,* but this realm has never been my home. I don't give a fuck what happens to it. Plus, you've made it *very* clear that you don't care what's important to me; why should I care what's important to *you*?"

The king's brows slammed down, and his lip curled. "Why must you be so difficult? I have just told you that you are to inherit this entire kingdom one day, and you act as if I have done you a great disservice. You may not have been born here, but you have always belonged to this realm. Now, this realm will belong to you, but you have to purify our bloodline. The fae will not stand for another race to rule over them."

"The fae themselves, or you?" Anevae asked.

"It is not just I who believes we are the superior race, Anevae. You will do well to remember that."

"And yet, the fae still rely on shifters and vampires to protect them. If they were truly superior, they wouldn't rely on the other races—they wouldn't trust anyone but their own kind. Pray tell, how many fae are amongst the guard that protect the castle?"

"That is *enough*. I will not stand for this any longer, especially this evening. You have continued to test my patience, to argue with me, and scrutinize the way of our people without even knowing them fully. Any other king who lived before me would not have stood for such horrid behavior, but I am not those kings. Adjust your attitude before I am forced to take action. I do not want to have to make an example out of you, but I will if I must."

Anevae stomped up the stairs to her suite, and I followed closely. When she reached the door, she threw it open and squealed. Rushing to look through the doorway, I watched as she flung herself into Cassiel's waiting arms.

"Are you okay?" he whispered.

"Her grandfather is being very... difficult right now," I said as I shut the door behind me.

Cassiel's eyes met mine, brows furrowed over his intense eyes. "What's that supposed to mean? Is he causing any major problems?"

Anevae unraveled herself from Cassiel's arms. "He's arranged a marriage between me and the Lord of Eirvanna's son... Amareon. But he's also made it known that I'm basically his last heir, unless he gets my mom to have more children, which won't be happening. Em, we need to figure out a way to speak with Amareon discreetly. I'll do as I'm told and get to know him, but there are always things that need to be discussed behind closed doors."

Walking up behind her, I wrapped my arms around her waist and pulled her flush to me. I moved her hair to the side and brushed my lips against her pulse point, loving the feel of it.

Her back arched into me as she whispered, "Bite me. I know you want to taste me again."

Huffing out a laugh, I kissed her neck again. "If I bite you, it's going to lead to other things. And I don't feel right making love to you while our mate is away from us."

She rested her head against my shoulder and sighed as she gazed into my eyes. Her mesmerizing baby blues sucked me into their ocean as they filled with tears and my heart shatter. I knew exactly how she felt because I felt it, too. My heart ached at every mention or thought of my missing mate.

I reached up to brush a tear away as it slid down her cheek. "We'll have her back soon. I promise."

Her voice broke as she asked, "How do you know?"

"I don't know for sure. But I have faith."

That night, before bed, we sat on the couches to unwind from the day.

Anevae joined me on one couch while Cassiel sat across from us. Once settled, I asked Cassiel, "Have you made it any further on the prophecy?"

Cassiel shook his head, rose to his feet, and disappeared. I fucking hated when he did that. He was back a minute later with the prophecy and the book he'd relied on the heaviest. Plopping back down on his couch, he placed everything on the table and turned it so I could see. All that was on the paper was what had been included with the prophecy when he received it:

A woman belonging to this realm... will unite the kingdom... She will be graced with a mate from each territory...

"I can't figure it out. I've learned absolutely *nothing* about the prophecy since I got it," he said, defeat evident in his voice.

"Any other leads on anyone who can help?" Anevae asked.

"Funny you should ask. The Librarian was a little weird when I visited the library in Baeruil. She asked about Anevae and Maeyve. Then she said Maeyve was 'taken back for a good reason.' When I asked her what that meant, she just told me I would understand why soon enough."

Anevae's confusion trickled through our bond as I worried my lip, trying to think of any good reason Maeyve would have to endure the life she ran from again. Then it dawned on me. "Anevae's last mate has to be in or near the brothel. That's the only 'good' reason I can think of for Maeyve to have been sent back. We know Anevae's last mate has to be from either Maiviraea or Kaeuil, right? Considering where we think the brothel may be, she can interact with plenty of demons and shifters."

Cassiel nodded, as if he was thinking over my speculation. "That would make sense. Has Maeyve reached out to you guys again? Have you or Anevae reached out like I keep suggesting?"

I shook my head and Anevae tensed beside me. "We're both a little scared. And Maeyve didn't even reach out when we communicated through our bond at dinner this evening. I'm not sure if she's found a way to shut us out or what, but I would've expected her to check on Anevae after dinner at least. I know you felt how powerful her emotions were—and you're not even mated to her yet—so there's no way Maeyve didn't feel it. I just hope she's okay."

"You would know if she wasn't. We have no clue what she has to endure while she's at the brothel, but she'll get through it. She's strong, hard-headed, and capable of taking care of herself; she proved that to everyone while she was alone in the woods for all those years. She'll make it back to us—alive—one way or another."

Letting out a heavy sigh, I said, "I guess you're right. Maybe we need to shift our focus to the puzzle piece before us—Amareon. The king claimed that Amareon isn't like Ambrose, but I'm still skeptical of him. Amareon *is* the twin to the fucker that hurt our mate, and I won't allow him to hurt her, too. Even if they're fated, I won't let Amareon lay a hand on our girl until we're sure of his intentions."

Cassiel's eyes flashed a glowing teal. "I agree. I'm not violent, but I won't ever let harm come to my mate, and I'll protect her with my life if it comes down to it."

Clenching my jaw, I wrapped an arm around Anevae's shoulders and kissed her head. "Good. We're on the same page about that, then. Tomorrow, we can figure out how to talk to Amareon privately. I think it's about time to head to bed."

With a yawn, Anevae agreed, and we climbed into the bed with Cassiel and I sandwiching our mate between us until it was time to face a new day.

Chapter Ten

Amareon

A sharp knock on my bedroom door startled me awake. When I rolled over, I found Maarya strolling in with a platter of food that smelled divine. Living in the castle would have its perks, for sure.

"Good morning, Lord Amareon. I have brought your breakfast. Your lessons with Cassiel will begin in an hour, so I will return shortly before that to escort you to the training room."

I rubbed my eyes and sat up to address her, but she was already walking out the door. Throwing the covers off, I scarfed down my food. Then I washed up and dressed in some casual clothing that was provided for me. My father had packed me a bag, likely knowing what the king was planning to do, but all he packed was formal clothing. He tried to impress upon me that being nobility meant we had to always look our best. Clearly, that went in one ear and out the other with me. Since I was just attending lessons, I wasn't worried about looking my best.

Maarya kept to her word, showing up about five minutes before my lessons were set to start. "I'm glad *someone* actually listens to me around here. Come, come. Let's get you to the training room."

With a small chuckle, I followed the slight faerie, keeping track of our route. Growing up, I'd come to the castle a handful of times, but was never allowed to wander the halls. Following Maarya, I realized why: the halls all looked identical, and a child could easily get lost. Hell, even an adult could get lost in this labyrinth. When we reached our destination, Maarya curtsied and was off again.

The voices of Anevae and her two consistent male companions filter through the open door of the training room, drawing my attention. The king had said he wanted me to attend lessons with Cassiel, but I didn't expect Anevae to be there. It would be smart and force us to become acquainted, even in the angel's presence and that of her vampire guard. But how would I talk to her about what I had felt—what Sameera and I spoke about—while the other two were there?

I took a deep breath. The best thing to do was to face things head-on. Taking a few steps inside, I glanced around, looking for the source of the voices. I reached the middle of the room before a cloth sack was thrown over my head. A massive hand clamped over my mouth so I couldn't scream, but left my nose unblocked so I could still breathe. My captor's other arm wrapped around me, pinning my arms to my sides as they dragged me backward and held me tightly as I thrashed in their arms.

Then, for a moment, I felt like I was floating before I was thrown onto a hard chair and my hands were tied behind my back. As I opened my mouth to speak, the sack covering my head was removed, startling me. Before me stood Anevae, flanked by her vampire guard, Emrhys, and an angel with massive black wings. The angel's muscular arms crossed his chest, lifting his shirt slightly to give me a peek of the V at his waistband. I couldn't help but stare at him and imagine what else was hiding under those clothes.

The vampire let out a laugh, recapturing my attention, and reached over to hit the angel playfully. "Looks like you have a new admirer, Cass."

The angel, now confirmed as Cassiel, rolled his eyes, and Anevae swayed side to side, clenching and unclenching her jaw. Just as the first time I'd seen her, I felt a pull to her I couldn't explain.

"Hey, fuckface. Eyes on me," Emrhys snapped.

"What the fuck is going on?" I asked, anger creeping into my voice.

Emrhys quirked an eyebrow. "What does it look like?"

"For fuck's sake, if you want to ask me questions, just ask them. You didn't have to tie me up," I said, glancing around to find that we were no longer in the training room but in someone's bedroom. "How the hell did we end up in here?"

"Conveyance," Cassiel said matter-of-factly.

"Why bring me here and not interrogate me in the training room?" I asked, still confused.

Anevae approached me cautiously, but confidently. "Too many of my grandfather's servants can't be trusted. They report back to him with anything suspicious, and this is my only safe space."

"Why tie me up, though?" I asked.

"For my comfort. I need to know you're nothing like your brother, because I can't go through that again. Especially if you are who we think you are," Anevae whispered with tears in her eyes.

"What did he actually do to you?" I asked hesitantly. "I know you hinted at things earlier, but..."

Anevae scoffed and wiped away the tears that threatened to escape. "The better question is, what *didn't* he do to me? He abused me in every way he could—mentally, emotionally, physically... sexually. I wasn't allowed to see my family or friends at one point. He constantly questioned my decisions and actions. He forced himself on me whenever he felt like it, and he beat me on several occasions. During a couple of those beatings, I lost consciousness, and he nearly killed me. A chance encounter with my sister is the only thing that saved me."

My mind spun as her words settled in. I knew my brother wasn't the best person, but I didn't realize how awful he truly treated others. "I almost wish your father hadn't killed him because I would've made his death as slow and painful as possible."

"You and me both," Emrhys growled from behind Anevae, his knuckles white and eyes a pulsing red.

On the other side of Anevae, Cassiel stood in a similar manner, his hands clenched and teal eyes aglow.

Anevae rolled her shoulders back and crossed her arms over her chest again. "It happened; it's in the past; and it's not happening *ever* again."

Emrhys approached Anevae from behind and placed his hands on her hips. "No one will ever hurt you again, my love." Then he kissed her temple and turned his attention back to me.

I'd suspected Emrhys and Anevae were together based on how protective the vampire was of Anevae, but my heart still stuttered at the sight of them being intimate.

Swallowing the lump in my throat, I said, "My mom raised Ambrose and me better than that, but my father greatly influenced the man my brother became. My father isn't known for treating others with the same respect he expects to be given. He was cruel to my mother. Seeing such cruelty affected my brother and me in completely opposite ways. Sameera, my mate—"

Anevae's eyes grew several sizes. "Did you say your mate? Like you're already mated?" When I nodded, she began pacing. "He can't be my fae mate if he's already mated. Can he?"

Cassiel stepped forward, blocking Anevae's path, and cupped her cheeks so she would look at him. "Emrhys and Maeyve are mated, too. It's possible that there can be multiple connections within the group. She could also be the last of your mates we have to find. Where is she, Amareon?"

"I've been trying to free her from a brothel in Western Maiviraea for the last eight years. My father is the one who's responsible for her being there."

Anevae broke free from Cassiel's grip and closed the distance between us. "A brothel in Western Maiviraea? Maeyve was taken to one there, too."

"Sameera contacted me the night before last. Maeyve is with her—they're roommates, actually—and they've felt the same telltale tingles of the mate bond."

"Why didn't you try to tell me sooner?" Anevae asked, brows furrowed.

"If you haven't noticed, I've had little time to speak with you since I've arrived. And in the time I've been able to, you've had me tied to a chair, and you've done most of the talking," I said, a little snippy.

In a blur of motion, Emrhys appeared behind me and loosened the ropes on my wrists. Pulling them free, I watched Anevae rise and take a few steps back toward her bed.

"I'm sorry," she whispered.

"You're not the one who tied me to a chair. It was one of these two," I said, gesturing toward Emrhys and Cassiel.

"Yeah, but I asked them to. Sometimes, just looking at you, I think of your brother. I have to break it down and remind myself of all the little differences," she said, eyes cast down to the floor.

My body moved of its own accord, strolling up to her. I reached out to lift her chin, even with the threatening snarl from Emrhys, and said, "Thank you."

One of her brows rose as she asked, "Why are you thanking me?"

"For seeing me as who I *am* instead of as who my brother *was* to you. It means a lot. The only other person who ever did that was my mom. My father has always wished I were more like my brother and couldn't appreciate that I'm able to bring something different to the table—that I'm my own person."

"I can't imagine how it feels," she whispered. "You might want to back away from me if you value your life, though. Emrhys is about ready to rip you to shreds. This was the first time they heard about what your brother put me through, and you're going to have to gain their trust."

A wide smile spread across my lips. "I'm not scared of the vampire. And I don't think the angel would hurt a thodwyn, even if it bit him."

Emrhys barked out a loud laugh, and Anevae's eyebrow rose again. Out of the corner of my eye, I caught sight of Cassiel's jaw tensing.

"With that face you're giving me, I'm going to guess you don't know what a thodwyn is," I said as I released her chin.

"Sure don't. But with how Emrhys is reacting, I'm guessing it's something super small or soft and cuddly," Anevae said.

Still grinning, Emrhys said, "Thodwyns are small bugs with wings that can bite, but rarely do. It stings pretty bad when they bite, though. They're similar, in a way, to what the humans call horse flies."

Anevae's face lit up. "Oh! I get it now. That's like when we say 'wouldn't hurt a fly' in the human realm. I need to learn so much more about this world."

Cassiel threw me a dirty look as he placed his hand on the small of Anevae's back. "You have plenty of time. I think we should head back down to the training room so we don't raise any suspicions."

With everyone in agreement, Cassiel grasped Anevae's hand and turned to me. Holding out a hand, he said, "It would be best if you came with us. Anyone who sees you leave Anevae's room would think it odd for you to exit, especially without her."

Knowing he was right, I took his hand. Tingles shot up my arm, distracting me from the incoming weightless feel.

Once the three of us were back on solid ground, I let go of Cassiel's hand and walked away from them. My mind was going a mile a minute. I'd already known touching Anevae would cause the tingling because it had already happened, but touching Cassiel caused them, too. While I'd never been thoroughly interested in dating men, everything about Cassiel drew me in. I didn't know how to think or feel about it and needed a minute to collect my thoughts.

Cassiel called out my name once... twice... and then a third time, but I didn't stop walking away from them. It wasn't until a massive hand grabbed my bicep, tingles surging through my arm, that I finally was able to force myself to stop.

"Where are you going?" Cassiel asked.

"I-I don't know. This is all too much right now."

"We're all figuring this out together. And you don't even know the half of it yet," the angel said with a breathy laugh.

When I met his gaze, his cheeks were a blazing red, and I sighed. "I can't take much more right now."

"Buckle up, buttercup. You're in for one hell of a ride, and it's only getting more complicated by the day," Emrhys said as he strolled past us.

With furrowed brows, Cassiel hissed, "You're not being very helpful right now, Em."

Emrhys scoffed. "When have you ever known me to be *that* helpful? Unless it comes to Anevae. Pretty boy here can learn to deal. It's not like the rest of us haven't."

"This is just a lot of information at once. How did you handle it, Cassiel?" I asked quietly.

"I didn't have much of a choice but to handle every bit of information as it has come. There are still times this situation becomes a little daunting, but it just feels right somehow. It does help that I heard about the prophecy we're investigating often while growing up. I feel like we'd understand some of the things we're facing if we could decipher it, though," Cassiel said.

"Why aren't you able to figure it out? Is it all in riddles?" I asked.

Cassiel shook his head. "It's in the ancient language that died out centuries ago. No one knows it anymore, and I've only found one book that could remotely help me, which isn't much at all."

My heart stuttered in my chest. "Maybe I came in at the perfect time, then. As a fae of nobility, my father felt it was important for me to know the ancient language."

Chapter Eleven

Maeyve

The first few days back at the brothel were excruciating, but I endured for my mates. Madam Tanith made no move to hide that she was trying to break me—make me think I'd never get out. She paired me with all of her most brutal clients, and I left every appointment beaten, bruised, and sore. But every night, I attended dinner and acted as if nothing was wrong. It irritated Madam Tanith greatly.

Sameera knew better, though. After seeing my last client on the first day, I stormed into our room, walking right past her to my dresser for a nightgown, and locked myself in the bathroom. I refused to let anyone see me break down in that place, including my potential mate. But when I came out of the bathroom and saw her still waiting on the bed, I couldn't hold it in anymore. Throwing my dirty clothes in the hamper, I crawled into my bed and let the tears spill. Sameera climbed into my bed with me and comforted me until I finally fell asleep.

By the third day of seeing the madam's hand-chosen clients, my entire body ached to the bone. My accelerated healing had slowed because I'd suffered far too many injuries in such a short time, so my body wasn't able to keep up. Nothing hurt worse than the separation from my mates, though.

The only thing keeping me safe and sane, for the most part, was Sameera. She had become my saving grace, especially when Anevae and Emrhys spoke to each other through our mate bond. Several times I wanted to respond—to make sure everything was okay—but I convinced myself not to; I didn't want my mates to worry about me. My philosophy had become that the less they heard from me, the less they had to worry about me. Deep down, I think I knew better. I struggled to shut them out, but I continued to remind myself that if they felt the pain being inflicted upon me, they would come for me blindly, likely leading to their demise.

On the morning of the third day, Sameera woke me by just whispering my name.

"Yes, love?" I said groggily, lifting my head from its spot on her chest. Even in my sleep, listening to her heart beating helped ground me. It reminded me that everything would be okay. Eventually.

Her hand rubbed circles on my back as she asked, "Why haven't you reached out to your mates? Or answered their attempts to reach out to you?"

I pushed myself up to look at her. "How do you know I haven't?"

"Amareon told me he's staying at the castle and has been speaking with them. He's apparently going to start working on the prophecy with Cassiel soon."

"Why would Amareon be helping Cassiel with the prophecy? It's written in the ancient language, and Cassiel hasn't been able to find anything to help. I don't—"

"Amareon knows the ancient language," Sameera said, a hopeful note in her voice.

I was stunned into silence. What were the odds that a member of the mate group would know the ancient language? If they figured the prophecy out, Sameera and I could find a way out of the brothel. Our mate group could finally become a complete unit.

Despite that, I was still concerned and fearful that things wouldn't go as they hoped. "Has he said anything else to you about it?"

"No. I haven't responded to him recently either. As you saw that first night, connecting with him hurts and can even leave me incapacitated for days if I try to do too much. It's been far too long since I've seen my mate, and our bond is suffering."

"Love, you can always tell me when you want to contact him, and I will help ease the pain. Just like the first time."

Sameera quirked her head slightly and asked, "How did you do that, anyway? Did you use your calming abilities?"

"Who told you about that?"

"Your mom told me all about you when I first got here, back when she thought you were dead. Have you talked to her since you've been here? I'm sure she'd love—"

"No. Absolutely not. I don't care how much she supposedly loved and cared about me. A mother who loves her child does *not* stand by while that child is forced to do things no child should *ever* have to do. My mother handed me over to the madam like I meant nothing to her, like I *was* nothing. I had to fend for myself for far too long because my mother focused all her attention on herself and the family she supposedly found here. Knowing everything I went through at her hands, I feel bad for those kids she has with her. I won't hesitate to take them if I find out she's no better to them than she was to me. They don't deserve the life I had."

Tears welled in Sameera's eyes. "I-I'm so sorry. I had no clue. She helped me acclimate to the brothel when I first got here. I wonder if maybe she was trying to do for me what she couldn't do for you as a child. Several times she told me how much I reminded her of you."

"I'm glad she helped you. And I hope she's changed for those kids."

"I think she has because she knew she didn't do her best for you... Or the others she's birthed since you left. The madam has basically been breeding her for the last fifty years," Sameera said, ending in a whisper.

"The madam has been doing *what?*" I asked, anger bubbling to the surface.

"I know you heard what I said."

"Why the fuck would the madam breed my mother?"

"She wants another you. For the last fifty years, everyone thought you were dead, and from what your mom has told me, you were the madam's prized possession. You made her the most successful, and she won't let anyone forget it."

"That's ridiculous! My mother told me she didn't even know who my father was, just that he was an incubus who couldn't seduce her. I'm not that special. There are plenty of others who can do a lot more than I can."

"While that may be true, she wants exactly what you do, which *does* make you special. You're also part of this incredible prophecy, saying you'll take part in uniting the kingdom again. I'd say that makes you pretty damn special, too."

Rolling my eyes, I put my head back down on her chest so I could listen to her heart again and calm down. After a few minutes, I asked, "How many kids has she had since I left?"

"I'm not sure of the exact number. Mordecai, the babe she's often seen cradling, was an accident. His father is a shifter who attacked your mom when she was in town getting some things for Marcelene, the little girl you see huddled close to your mom. The madam has been dictating everything. She only wants girls, and thankfully, that's all there's been until Mordecai. After each baby is born, the madam watches to see what powers the girl develops. If the girl's powers aren't up to par, she forces your mom to have another baby. I've only been around for Marcelene and Mordecai thus far."

"What happened to the girls that weren't 'up to par' according to the madam's standards?"

"I'm not sure if your mom distances herself from the girls once they're gone or what, but she never talks about them."

90

"Stupid fucking bitch. I want to kill the madam even more now than I did before. My mom may not have been the best, but she doesn't deserve to be bred like a damn animal."

Still seething, my mind block fell, and Anevae was immediately there, panicking. *Maeyve. Baby. Are you okay? What's going on?*

I took a few deep breaths before replying. *I'm fine, my love. I just learned something about my mom and the madam that's getting to me.*

It's so good to hear your voice, Anevae said, relief flooding our bond.

It's great to hear yours as well, I said, my heart breaking because I knew I'd have to put my block back up before I left the bedroom.

"What's wrong?" Sameera asked at the same time as Anevae asked, *Why are you in so much pain?*

"I fucked up and my mates—well, Anevae at least—felt my anger and can now feel my pain. She's trying to make sure I'm okay, but I can't keep our bond open much longer. Neither of them can continue to feel everything I do," I said as a tear slid down my cheek onto Sameera's shirt.

Sameera rubbed her hand up and down my back again. "I understand. I've been there. Talk to her for a few minutes; it may help you take your mind off everything happening here."

Nodding, I replied to Anevae, *I'm fine, my love. Sameera told me Amareon's at the castle with you guys.*

Don't go trying to change the subject, Emrhys said, chiming in finally.

A small smile graced my lips for the first time in a while. *There you are. I'm amazed you kept your thoughts to yourself for that long.*

Haha. Very funny, Emrhys said. *I'm serious, though. Why are you in so much pain, little fox?*

I let out a long sigh and willed my body to relax, trying to dull the pain so they didn't feel it as much. *I don't want to talk about it right now. I'm due downstairs soon, and I'd rather know how things are going on your end.*

Emrhys made sure to filter his annoyance through the bond, and I rolled my eyes. I wouldn't have expected it from anyone else, though.

Enough, Anevae said, likely glaring at Emrhys if they were in the same room. *Yes, Amareon is here and will be helping Cassiel work on the prophecy. We're working on getting you and Sameera out of there as soon as possible. Just... hold on a little longer.*

We've got this, my love, I said, trying to sound confident even though I wasn't sure how much more physical abuse my body could take. But I told them I would get out of the situation I was in on my own, and even though it was a little more complicated than it started out, I still had every intention of doing so.

I know you do, but I don't like it. I want you back with me. Where you belong, Anevae said.

Soon enough, I will be, but right now, I have to go. I need to grab something to eat before I get the day started. I love you both.

I love you, too, both of my mates said simultaneously.

Sameera and I dragged our feet to get downstairs. Neither of us was seeing clients until later in the morning, and with the new information I'd been given about my mother, I didn't want to come face to face with her. I still loathed her, but what she was going through was unimaginable—horrible, really. Like I'd told Sameera, no one deserved to be treated like that. I couldn't stand by and watch it either. It made me sick.

As we descended the stairs, my mother exited the kitchen with little Mordecai in her arms and Marcelene at her heels. When she spotted me, she stopped dead in her tracks, and Marcelene ran into her. Marcelene followed our mother's line of sight, and the moment she realized I was there, she hid behind our mother.

I didn't realize I'd also stopped until someone cleared their throat behind me. Whispering an apology, I hurried down the stairs and out of the way, with Sameera close behind me. My mother and I stood there, eyes glued to each other. She looked almost exactly as she did when I'd left Caellaias, which was to be expected, seeing as she was only nearing two hundred years old. But she'd started developing wrinkles around her eyes and forehead—I wondered if having so many children could age women like that. Not only that, but she looked miserable. The handful of times I'd seen her since my return, she hadn't smiled once. And behind her once vibrant amber eyes, there was no spark left.

Before I knew what I was doing, I was across the room, throwing my arms around her from the side so I didn't suffocate Mordecai. "I'm sorry, Mom," I whispered into her hair, catching hints of her vanilla and berry scent behind the floral soap Madam Tanith forced us to use.

"Oh, sweetheart, you have nothing to be sorry for. I'm the one who has wronged you in more ways than I can count. You did what you had to do to stay alive, and I've done what I've had to. I've made some questionable choices along the way, and I'm sorry for everything you went through because of those choices."

"I'm going to get you out of here. And I'll make the madam pay for everything she's done over the years. I promise. Until then, keep doing what you have to, but please don't put these kids in harm's way like you did to me," I said, voice cracking several times.

"Be careful, Vee. She's more powerful than you think," my mom warned.

As I let her go, I said, "I've got this, Mom. I'm not the timid, obedient girl I used to be." Then I walked off toward the kitchen.

After grabbing food, I sat at one of the dining room tables, and Sameera joined me

"What the fuck was that? I thought you wanted nothing to do with her," she hissed.

"I know. She's still my mom, though. As much as I hate what she put me through, I refuse to stand by and watch her be treated like livestock. Mordecai and Marcelene need a home that this place can't provide."

"That's understandable. But how the fuck are you going to get her out of here? As long as the madam is alive, your mom won't be leaving this place."

When I finished chewing, I smirked. "Who said the madam would be alive when my mom leaves?"

Chapter Twelve

Cassiel

When Amareon told us he knew the ancient language, I was ecstatic. Hope blossomed in my chest for the first time during the disaster of a situation we were stuck in. With him knowing the ancient language, we might finally work out the prophecy and get our girls back to us. The only thing—well, being—standing in our way was the king, and we had no idea how to manage the problems he posed for us yet. But that was a problem for later.

Now that we had someone capable of deciphering it, and Anevae and Emrhys had been in contact with Maeyve, we needed to get to work on the prophecy. Between Emrhys asking a million questions and Anevae's persistent anxiety, we weren't going to make much progress on it with them hovering around. So I invited Amareon to my room after dinner the following night, so we had the ability to focus.

While I waited for him, I began laying everything out on the coffee table, just as I'd done every time I'd worked on the prophecy. As I set everything up, a wave of disappointment washed over me. After the countless hours I'd spent working on the prophecy, I still had so little to show for it.

A knock on the door told me my guest had arrived. An unusual fluttering in my chest had me feeling anxious as I strode to the door to greet him. When I pulled it open, Amareon's stunning smile had my heart racing. Gods, was he gorgeous. It was a new experience for me—having feelings for one being, let alone two.

"Good evening, Cassiel," Amareon said in his deep, silky voice, pulling me from my thoughts.

"Good evening, Amareon. Thank you for joining me. Please come in," I said, stepping aside so he could enter.

With a whispered thanks, he bowed his head and ambled past me. His delicious scent followed and I wanted to bask in it. As was typical for the fae, his scent was floral, but his dark, earthy undertones drew me in even further. And, just as with Anevae from the first moment I saw her, I wanted nothing more than to let him consume me from the inside out.

Everything I was thinking and feeling around him was odd. I didn't know what to think of it.

Pulling myself from my dark, dirty, odd thoughts, I took a deep breath and shut the door before walking toward the couch. "Everything I have regarding the prophecy has been laid on the table for you to review. I'm sad to say I have little to show for all the work I put into it." I sighed, disappointed in myself. "The elders didn't teach me the ancient language when I was young. You would think they would've with as old as I am."

Amareon's smile deepened to show off his sparkling white teeth as he approached me. "I find it kind of cute when you ramble. Are you nervous about something?"

An intense heat crept across my cheeks. "It appears I am and I'm, uh, not quite sure why."

Stopping about a foot before me, Amareon threw his head back and laughed loudly. When his gaze returned to mine, his eyes had become hooded, and his pupils were blown so wide you could barely see his irises. "I don't think you're just nervous, Cassie. You're flustered and have something on your beautiful mind other than the task at hand."

I rolled my bottom lip between my teeth and let my gaze wander down his chest. I'd never been so attracted to another male in my entire life, but this one was going to be trouble for me in the worst possible way. With as close as he'd gotten to me, his scent completely engulfed me, making it impossible to think about anything but him.

Confusion swirled through my mind. Being an angel, I didn't have the intensified sense of smell like shifters and vampires, so scents rarely got to me. Even with Anevae, her scent never got as overpowering as Amareon's was at that moment. Then, it hit me. Voice deeper and huskier than normal, I asked, "How long did you say you've been without your mate?"

"I didn't say. Why does it matter?" Amareon asked, trying with all his might to keep himself rooted in the same spot.

"Have you been intimate with anyone else since she's been gone?"

Amareon's brows slammed down. "Of course I haven't. Again, why does this matter?"

"We're both fated to Anevae, and we've seen that there can be other mate bonds within the group. After I held your hand during the conveyance, I'm certain we're able to mate. According to my research on fated mates, when a mated pair stays apart for too long, then are reunited, the bond does whatever it can to draw their mate in again. I believe that your bond is currently using a tactic called scent bombing. Now that your bond has sensed Anevae and me, it wants one of us to satiate it."

Taking a step back, Amareon crossed his arms over his chest. "This wasn't happening at dinner with Anevae."

"Her family was around, and she's not open to your presence yet."

"If she's the central point of our bond group, why would it be happening with you?"

"You can't deny there's already an attraction between us. I saw the way your gaze devoured me the first time we met. You can't keep your eyes off me when we're in the same room, and your bond has picked up on that."

"How do I stop this?" he asked, trying to take a step back.

I huffed out a laugh. "Well, one way to calm it down is by putting ample space between you and your fated mate. That's kind of hard to do with Anevae right now. Especially since you're supposed to be getting to know each other, and if the king gets what he wants, you'll be married in a little over a week and a half."

"Well, that clearly won't be happening if I don't want to piss off the king. Is there anything else I can do?"

"The only other way to control it is to... satisfy it."

Amareon's brow rose. "Satisfy it? And how does one *satisfy* a mate bond?"

I gave him a smirk and leaned against the arm of the couch. "I think you know the answer to that."

Stepping up to me again, he whispered, "Humor me, Cassie. What can I do to satisfy it?"

My heart raced as I brushed a stray eyelash from his cheek. The possibility of having another mate when I wasn't even supposed to have the first scared me. I didn't learn about love and sex growing up—I never even learned about how other beings mated. As I got older, I discovered angels only had sex when the elders chose them to bring in a new generation. Other than that, the council forbade it.

Just as I was about to touch Amareon's cheek, he grabbed my wrist. Tingles snaked their way up my arm, and his resolve snapped. Before I could take another breath, his lips were on mine, and his scent enveloped me again. That was all it took for my body to take over, and I snaked my free hand around the small of his back so I could pull him flush against me.

Amareon let out a low growl and deepened the kiss, slipping his tongue past my parted lips. I groaned and gripped his shirt as my dick twitched, hitting the solid muscle of his thigh. I needed him to do *something.*

Anevae was the first person I'd ever had sex with. Even then, I only knew what to do because I'd watched Emrhys take her before me. Having sex with another male would be completely different, and I hoped to any god listening that Amareon was better versed than I was.

When he finally pulled back, he released my wrist and gazed into my eyes. An undercurrent of electricity pulsed between us as we breathed heavily, trying to catch our breath.

Breaking the silence, I said, "I-I've never done... *this*," and gestured between us.

Amareon's cheeks flushed a bright red. "Neither have I. But we'll figure it out. If this is something you want to explore, that is."

Relaxing my grip on his shirt, I rubbed the small of his back. "Would I have pulled you closer if I didn't want to keep going?"

"Well, no. I guess not."

Then I grabbed his hand and had to stop for a moment because an intense tingling wave shot through my body. My dick twitched again, bringing me back to the moment, so I brought Amareon's hand down to feel how he affected me. "Would my dick be this hard if I didn't want you?"

"I mean, my scent—"

"It's not just your scent drawing me in. It's you as a whole."

"Thank fuck, because I don't know what I would've done if you didn't want me. Fuck, Cass... I haven't felt this way about anyone since Sameera. Don't get me wrong, I have an intense pull toward Anevae, but so far it's completely different from how I feel about you and Sameera."

A half smile pulled up the corner of my lips. "I think you feel that way with me because your bond is determined to connect with the most available mate, which happens to be me at the moment. When Anevae opens up to you and there's no one in your way to claim her, I have no doubt you'll feel that instant pull to be with her like the rest of us have."

Amareon stroked my hard length over the thick fabric of my pants and said, "While I hope that's the case, right now, all I can focus on is how hard you are and how much I want to please you. I want to wrap my lips around your cock and bring you pleasure while your hands tangle in my hair. Then, I want you to lose control and fuck my mouth until your cum coats my tongue and all I can taste is you for the rest of the night."

"Fuck me," I whimpered as my dick twitched against his hand. All the dirty things coming from his mouth had my heart beating out of my chest. I'd only ever heard Emrhys talk to Anevae and Maeyve that way. No one had ever directed those sentiments toward me, but I loved it coming from his lips.

Amareon licked his lips before asking, "Is that an invitation? Or a request?"

"I, uh, I'm not even sure at this point. You've got me so damn hard I can't even think straight."

He laughed as he pulled me to stand and claimed my lips again. When we parted, he sank to his knees and slipped his fingers in the waistband of my pants. From the floor, he looked up at me with his mismatched eyes, seeking permission to continue. I nodded vigorously, and he smiled wider.

Amareon bit his lip as he unfastened the button on my pants. I struggled to remain still, gripping the arm of the couch behind me to keep myself from helping him. When my pants were fully opened, he pulled them down my hips. Once they hit the floor, he played with the hem of my boxers, getting dangerously close to touching where I desperately wanted him.

My cock was already begging for his attention. "I swear to the gods you're torturing me."

"And you're loving every fucking second of it. Aren't you, Cassie?" he teased and licked his lips like a starved animal about to feast on its long-awaited meal.

"Fuck, Mare. Yes, I do. But I would love it even more if you would stop teasing me."

"Aww. The big soft angel doesn't enjoy being teased."

Removing one of my hands from the couch, I grabbed a handful of his shaggy blonde hair and pulled his head back. Then I leaned down and moved to kiss him, but instead I bit his lip hard. When I released it, I said, "If you're not careful, I'm going to throw you onto my bed and fill your ass with my cum instead. While I can be patient, I can't wait to fuck you right now. Whether it's your mouth or your ass is up to you."

I was astonished at my words, but Amareon and his bond's desperation made me absolutely feral. Even when I had sex with Anevae for the first time, I hadn't felt like I did with Amareon. My bond was reacting to his and dying to claim him as mine.

With a gleam in his eye, Amareon bit his lip and slipped my boxers down to my feet. When they hit the floor, my dick bobbed, growing impatient. Amareon took his time, trailing one of his hands up my thigh to my hip while the other palmed my length, stroking me perfectly from root to tip. A small moan escaped my lips as he used his thumb to swipe the bead of pre-cum that leaked from my tip and brought it to his lips, sucking it into his mouth.

Removing his thumb with a pop, he said, "You taste even better than you smell   so sweet and smoky. Well, of course, a little salty, but it's the perfect combination."

My grip on his hair loosened, and he lowered his head to lick up my length. I sharply inhaled, my whole body tensing as I damn near lost it.

"Fuuuuuck, Mare. I—" I started, but that's when he took me into his mouth. My eyes rolled into the back of my head, and my hand gripped his hair tighter.

He pushed back against my grip until just my tip was in his mouth. Then he grabbed my ass tight and sucked my dick down until I nearly made him gag. My hold on his hair tightened, making it hard for him to continue, but he did, repeating his movements as I threw my head back and filled the room with my moans.

When my balls began tightening, Amareon popped off my dick, and I let out a frustrated grunt. He squeezed my ass and looked up at me with a smirk. "Patience. I think you'll enjoy this."

Confused, I loosened my hold on his hair, watching as he brought one of his hands to his lips and plunged two fingers into his mouth to soak them with his spit. His eyes didn't leave mine when he slid his fingers out of his mouth and returned his mouth to my impatient cock, licking up the underside. I threw my head back and tangled my hand in his hair again, completely forgetting about his hand until I felt his digits start circling my puckered hole.

Popping off me again, he whispered, "Relax."

Doing as he said, he sucked me back into his mouth while one of his fingers worked its way into my ass. The intrusion was uncomfortable at first, but as his finger plunged further in, he hit a spot that had my toes curling and my back bowing. He slowly pumped in and out, warming me up until he could add the other. When he did, he sped up his movements on both fronts, and I saw stars.

"I-I'm gonna," I said, trying to warn him, but he just increased his pace, and I couldn't hold on anymore. An orgasm ripped through me so hard I thought I was going to pass out. Amareon's hands on me were the only thing that kept me upright.

My fingers disentangled from his hair, and my hand dropped to the arm of the couch again as I watched Amareon swallow and wipe his mouth off with the back of his hand. Then, he rose and captured my lips, slipping his tongue in to caress mine and claim me all over again. A satisfied moan slipped past my lips when we separated.

"You did so well and gods, you taste so fucking divine, but I guess that's to be expected with you being an angel," Amareon whispered before walking to the sink so he could wash his hands.

I stood there, unable to move, as I watched him walk off. For the first time, I allowed myself to look him over in full. He was pretty tall for a fae—at least six feet four—and had muscles for days. His wavy, blonde hair was so shiny that when the light hit it just right, it reminded me of the polished gold I'd seen from the human realm.

And even though I'd just had my fingers tangled in the strands, you couldn't even tell it'd been disheveled in the least.

"Are you just going to stand there and stare at me with your pants around your ankles?" he asked, looking at me in the mirror.

My cheeks reddened, and I reached down to pull up my pants and boxers. After fastening them, I leaned back against the arm of the couch, crossing my arms over my chest. A hint of a smile peeked at me in the mirror just before Amareon turned around to face me. His hungry gaze settled on me, and I rolled my eyes. Inadvertently, my eyes raked down his body. The wet spot on the front of his pants caught my attention, and when my eyes made their way back to his, I raised an eyebrow.

"It's exactly what it looks like. You didn't even have to touch me to make me come," he said, pushing off the sink to make his way back to me.

"Interesting. It looks like you still want more, though," I said, teasing.

"I don't think I could get enough of you," he said, stepping up to me.

Uncrossing my arms, I slid them under his shirt and pulled him close. "I know I won't be able to get enough of you anytime soon. That was incredible."

With a smile, he moved to kiss me, but I pulled him flush against me and our mouths collided in a passionate kiss. His hand slid around my neck, gripping the back of it possessively. Then, an unfamiliar warmth spread across my neck and down one of my arms.

Amareon jumped back, breaking our kiss. Each of us grimaced in pain, and our hands shot to the exact spot the other had touched.

"What the fuck was that?" Amareon asked.

I took a deep breath, willing the pain in my neck to calm, but nothing happened. "I have no clue, but my neck burns."

"My side feels like it's on fire," he said as he raised his shirt to try to look at it.

Glancing at his exposed skin, I gasped and forgot all about my neck.

Chapter Thirteen

Anevae

Emrhys insisted we get ready for bed while I waited for Cassiel, but my sweet angel still wasn't there by the time I was done. I was thoroughly displeased when Cassiel insisted that he and Amareon look over the prophecy alone in his room because I desperately wanted to be there with them, to see what they found. But I took solace in knowing he would tell me everything they discovered when he came to my room that night.

Unable to sit still, I paced across the room, anxious about what they'd find. Emrhys watched me patiently for a while before I finally let him drag me to bed. When we got settled, he wrapped me up in his arms, my back to his front, but my mind was still racing. Apparently, so was my heart.

"He'll be here soon enough. Get some rest, baby," Emrhys whispered in my ear.

"I know. I just don't sleep well when he's not here."

Emrhys nuzzled in and pulled me closer. "Would you like me to whisper sweet nothings in your ear to distract you? Or I can give you an orgasm to relax you, even a little."

Despite the war taking place in my head, my pussy throbbed. He hadn't touched me since before Maeyve was taken, and my body desperately wanted him.

He placed sweet, methodical kisses on my neck and moved to my ear. Taking the lobe gently between his teeth, he tugged lightly, and a moan slipped past my parted lips. His breathy laugh filled my ear before releasing it and kissing down my neck again.

When I moved to roll onto my back, he positioned himself between my parted legs and said, "Gods, I'm so fucking lucky. You're so damn beautiful. So fucking perfect."

With a dramatic rolling of my eyes, I tried to reach for him, but he grabbed my wrists and pinned them above my head. An intense fire burned in his ruby red eyes as he stared down at me. I knew exactly what he wanted without even needing to say a word.

"Have your way with me, Em," I whispered.

"Oh, I will. I guess it's a good thing you chose this skimpy little nightgown," he said just before he bent down to suck my nipple into his mouth with the thin fabric of my nightgown.

Letting the hardened peak slip from between his lips, he kissed up my chest to my neck. I moved my head to the side, exposing my flesh, and waiting for him to bite me. Instead, he kissed down my shoulder again, stopping at the strap of my nightgown. I wasn't sure what he was doing, but I'd told him to have his way with me, so I was just along for the ride at that point.

And I was enjoying every single second of it.

"Em," I whimpered out his nickname, wishing he'd stop teasing me.

Lifting his head, he asked, "You like this, princess?"

I rolled my eyes. "Do I really need to answer that question?"

"No. I could always stroke your pretty pussy to see how wet you are, but I still like hearing you tell me you're enjoying yourself," he said. Then his grip on my wrists changed. One of his massive hands wrapped around them both so he could trail the other to my shoulder.

As if it were nothing, he snapped the strap of my nightgown, and I hissed, "Hey! What did you do that for?"

He gave me one of those devastating smiles that showed off his fangs. His hungry, red eyes never left mine as he pulled down the fabric to reveal my bare breast. Licking his lips, he lowered his lips to kiss my bare skin. He was silently daring me to fight him, but instead, I bit my lip and watched him make his way to my nipple—the one he marked, claiming me as his. His tongue circled the stiff peak, lightly jostling the jewelry adorning it. I let out a gasp and arched my back.

I pulled at my hands, which he still held above my head, desperately wanting to reach for him. When he didn't let go, I whimpered, "Please. I need to touch you."

Releasing my nipple, he said, "Maybe, if you're a good girl, I'll let you." Then he kissed up to the sensitive spot behind my ear and whispered, "Right now, I'm going to let go of your hands—because I don't have enough fucking hands of my own—and you're going to keep them just like this. If they move even an inch, I will bring you to the brink of orgasm and leave you begging me for more while I flip you over to spank your ass so hard you won't be able to sit for weeks."

I had never been edged before, but I'd heard the orgasm afterward was more intense. And I was a sucker for a good spanking after Maeyve introduced me to it. "That doesn't sound like much of a punishment to me."

He brought his lips to hover just over mine, and I tried to sit up to kiss him. But he tsked and slid his free hand down my body until it slipped between my legs. He ran his fingertips ever so lightly over my slit before spreading me open and plunging two fingers into my soaking wet center. Pumping in and out a few times, he watched me squirm with a satisfied smile.

"Already so wet for me," he said as he withdrew his fingers and brought them to my lips. "Let me see your tongue, princess." I happily obliged, sticking my tongue out as far as I could. "Good girl," he whispered, sticking his fingers into my mouth and demanding, "Now, clean them off."

I closed my lips around his fingers and swirled my tongue around them to lap up every last drop of my arousal. Then I hollowed out my cheeks as he freed his fingers from my mouth.

"Fuck. If only you were doing that to my cock," Emrhys said, voice husky as he stared at me with those starved eyes.

"Let go of my hands, and I can give you exactly what you want."

"That sounds quite tempting, but I like my original idea a little better right now."

I rolled my eyes and wiggled impatiently. "Then get on with it before I get bored."

Emrhys' hand was on my throat before I could take my next breath. "You better be careful with that mouth of yours. It's asking for a punishment right now, and I'm more than happy to oblige by shoving my cock so deep into your throat that you can't breathe."

I raised my brow and licked my bottom lip before biting one of my piercings. "I rather enjoy punishments from you. Especially ones like that one."

"What am I going to do with you?" he asked with a smirk. Then he was on his feet in a flash. I tried to follow his movements, but he was so damn fast I couldn't keep up.

When I tried to sit up to look for him, he was back above me, tsking. "I told you that you weren't allowed to move. I guess it's a good thing I found this in your armoire," he said, holding up a scarf my grandfather had bought for me, which I knew I'd never wear. My eyes widened and my wetness slicked the inside of my thighs when he demanded, "Give me your hands."

Slowly, I brought my wrists to his waiting hands and watched as he tied them into an intricate knot. Once the last knot was tied, he yanked my hands over my head and secured the scarf to one of the bedposts.

My mouth fell open, speechless for a moment as I stared back up at him. When I found my voice again, I said, "I don't know whether I love or hate you right now."

Emrhys barked out a laugh and then bent down until our lips almost touched. "You're going to love this; I promise. Now, just sit back, relax, and enjoy the *ride*, princess."

When the last word left his lips, he consumed me, kissing me until I couldn't breathe. The loss of his lips on mine was devastating at first. Until he began kissing down my neck and chest, undressing me more along the way. By the time he reached my panty line, all my clothes were off and they'd been torn to shreds.

"Maybe I should start sleeping naked so you don't ruin any more of my clothes," I grumbled.

Emrhys' eyes fixed on me from between my parted legs, where he'd settled. "Where's the fun in that? This is all foreplay, and we all know that's one of the things you love most."

"I've had to beg and plead for my damn underwear because I still refuse to go commando." Emrhys' eyebrow raised, and I let out a groan. "I refuse to walk around not wearing underwear."

"You don't like the breeze caressing your bare skin underneath those dresses? I bet it feels fucking amazing." And like the tease he was, he blew on my clit, making me squirm under his gaze.

I burst into a fit of giggles until he stopped. "I don't know if that tickles or feels good. Maybe a bit of both?"

"It's good to hear you laugh a little. Too bad my primary goal this evening is to make you come on my face so hard, all you can do is scream."

"If that's really your goal, then you better get on with it before Cassiel gets here. Unless you're willing to share me."

Emrhys' signature smirk flitted across his lips, and I swore his eyes flickered black momentarily. Then, he stuck out his tongue and licked up my slit, ending on the sensitive bundle of nerves where he flattened his tongue and circled several times.

I moved to wrap my legs around his head, but his hands pinned them down, squeezing my thighs tightly. "I knew I should've tied these down too. You're being a naughty girl, not listening to my instructions."

"You only told me I couldn't move my hands. You never said anything about my legs or my feet."

Shaking his head, he said, "I guess you're right. Here's the warning now, though—your arms and legs don't move an inch until I say so."

"Yes, *daddy*," I whispered.

A growl between my thighs was the only warning I got before Emrhys sucked my clit into his mouth and bit down on the sensitive flesh. My eyes slammed shut, and my back bowed off the bed as the instant heat from his bite had an orgasm ripping through me, making me want to scream louder than ever.

As if someone could read my mind, a hand clamped down over my mouth to stifle my screams. The tingling trickling down my neck to the rest of my body let me know it was one of my mates, but I wasn't sure which one because of the orgasm still sending shockwaves through me. It didn't help that my eyes were still sealed shut either.

Emrhys' tongue continued languid strokes across my clit while he drank from me, and I was a shaking mess by the time my orgasm began to fade. I squirmed against his hold, my sensitive clit needing a reprieve from his tongue, but his grip on me tightened, and I couldn't help the whimper from deep within me.

A quiet laugh, unfamiliar to me, had my eyes flying open. Above me, with his hand still covering my mouth, was Amareon. The very last person I expected, even though his room was across from Emrhys' down the hall. His heated gaze swept up and down my naked form, and I screamed against his hand, flailing with the most miserable attempt because of Emrhys' hold, as a sly grin appeared on his face.

"This is why I haven't taken my hand off your mouth yet. I knew you'd react this way," Amareon said.

Emrhys pinned my legs against the bed to keep me still and withdrew my clit from his mouth so he could close the wound. When he moved to sit up, he wiped the back of his hand across his mouth, removing the mix of my arousal and blood just so he could lick it up again.

"I was right that your blood and pussy taste divine together. Fuck, I won't be able to get enough of that. *Ever*," Emrhys said with a playful smile.

Trying to wrench my legs from his grip, I cussed him out in my head, since Amareon still had a hand over my mouth. *Untie me and let me get dressed. Now. Why the fuck is he here? Where's Cassiel?*

Emrhys let out a sigh. "Amareon, take your hand off her mouth and move. She's not going to scream again; you just startled her. Princess, Cassiel is behind Amareon. If he'd stop hovering over you, you'd be able to see him. I assume they're both here because they discovered something."

When he finished speaking, Amareon removed his hand from my mouth, and Emrhys came down on top of me to give me a quick kiss. Through our bond, he asked, *My question for you is, why would I want you to get dressed? I'm not done with you. The other two are just as hot for you as I am, and I'm sure they'd join in on bringing you more pleasure. You belong to us just as much as we belong to you. I know you don't trust Amareon yet—neither do I—but he's here whether we like it or not. I think I'd like to leave you tied up for a while and show off your body to these two.*

"Don't you fucking dare, Em," I hissed.

The fucker smiled and then pushed himself off the bed, walking toward the makeshift bathroom. I tried to pull on my scarf, but it didn't budge, so I tried to scoot up, but my legs were still like jello. Whipping my head to the side, I found Amareon and Cassiel holding hands and just staring at me.

"Do y'all think you can help me, please?" I asked, trying to sound sweet, but I knew I sounded snippy.

"Don't. Leave her there to look at. I rather like her like this," Emrhys said as he strolled over to sit on the bed again. The moment he sat, I kicked my foot out. With his quick reflexes and speed, he caught it as if I were barely moving. "That wasn't very nice, now was it?"

"At least fucking cover me up. I'm uncomfortable being like this with... him in here," I said through gritted teeth.

Emrhys sat there, staring at me, seemingly unfazed by my confession. I stared right back at him, jaw set, until Cassiel cleared his throat beside us.

When neither of us looked at him, Cassiel untied the scarf from the headboard and scooped me into his arms. "Emrhys, I know you're trying to assert dominance or whatever, but she's uncomfortable, and you should take that seriously. I'm taking Anevae to the bathing chamber so she can get dressed. Amareon and I have something to share with you both."

Once in the bathing chamber, it took everything in me not to start crying. He took a minute to get me some clean clothes, then my sweet angel stood by as I cleaned up and got dressed. His gaze continuously drifted up and down my naked body, but it didn't bother me. He'd made it clear that his biggest priority was making sure I was safe and comfortable before anything else.

After sliding on the nightgown Cassiel provided me, I sauntered to where he stood, placed my hands on his chest, and got on my tiptoes to kiss him. "Thank you," I whispered.

His massive hands cupped my face, pulling me in for one more kiss before stroking my bottom lip with his thumb. "You never have to thank me for taking care of you. It doesn't matter what way, shape, or form it's in. I love you, Anevae. I'll do anything for you."

Chapter Fourteen

Amareon

Arms crossed, I watched as Cassiel carried Anevae behind the screens of the bathing chamber. Watching her fall apart when Emrhys bit her had my cock aching again. I had a feeling she wouldn't be happy about me covering her mouth, but I could see how hard she was fighting the scream from her orgasm. My decision was validated when she screamed a second time, startled by my presence. We couldn't risk her drawing enough attention to have the guards storming her room.

"Probably wasn't the best idea for you and Cass to pop in here unannounced," Emrhys said as he readjusted himself, his obvious erection likely as excruciating as mine was.

"That was all Cassie's doing. He's really excited and couldn't wait to tell Anevae what we learned. We couldn't have known what you two were doing until we got here. Cassie said neither of you has touched Anevae since the king sent Maeyve away," I said with a shrug.

"It seems Cass has a new nickname. I like it." He pauses. "I don't care if either of you watches us or looks at her when she's naked, but she's still not comfortable with you doing either of those things. I don't know how to rectify that aside from letting her adjust. It's only day two, but we don't have much time. Did you guys decipher the prophecy *already*?"

I shook my head and scoffed at myself. "We didn't even start on the prophecy. My bond apparently doesn't want me to keep my dick in my pants."

Emrhys' eyes bore into me. Absent-mindedly, I rubbed my side, and my shirt rode up. He grasped my shirt, pulling it up to look at the new mark on my skin.

"What the fuck is this?" he asked, concern lacing his voice.

"It's the reason we came here so quickly. That's all I want to say until Anevae and Cassiel return," I said with a glare.

He released me and stomped to the couch before throwing himself on it. I turned my attention to where Cassiel stood with his back to me. His posture was completely different in the comfort of Anevae's bedroom than anywhere else, even in his own quarters. In the short time I'd spent with the three of them, it was evident that Cassiel was head over heels for Anevae. But I could see why; she was a beacon for him. One of hope. Of love. Of a future he never thought possible.

Even with that knowledge, a tinge of jealousy surged, but I tamped it back down. I hadn't been around for long enough to be concerned about it. The thing that still ate at me though was that the first thing he said after we found the mating marks was that he originally envisioned Anevae would be his first mate. Of course, hearing that from him hurt more than I could express. It'd been so long since I'd had Sameera in my arms that having someone to bring me comfort again, the way only she could, made me feel so hopeful that things would be alright.

I love you, kitten; I can't wait to finally be able to do something right for once and get you out of that place. We're working on it. I promise, I said to my faraway mate, not even sure if she'd be able to hear me due to how tightly she locked down her bond.

To my surprise, her quiet voice carried into my mind, *I love you, too. Is everything okay? You feel a little off.*

I'm sorry you can feel it. Things have changed since last we spoke. Cassiel and I accidentally mated this evening. We haven't told the others yet, but will be doing so soon and I'm nervous. I'm an outsider here and Anevae barely trusts me as it is. It makes me miss you more than ever. I can't wait to have you in my arms again, I explained.

I'm sorry. Maeyve and I can hold our own for now. We'll be with you all soon, she said just before she closed our bond.

With a heavy breath, I refocused on Cassiel. He'd just spun around with Anevae's hand in his and was walking toward the couches. When our eyes met, a stunning smile graced his lips. But then he noticed something was wrong and pulled Anevae with him to where I stood.

As he approached, I said, "I'm fine. I just miss my mate right now."

His brows furrowed, and he turned to Anevae. Bringing his hands to her face, he gently kissed her lips and forehead. "Why don't you go see what's going on with Em? His lying face down on that damn couch could be several things. I need to talk to Amareon for a moment. We'll join you over there shortly."

"I can do that. Amareon, I'm sorry that I've had such a harsh reaction to you every time I've seen you. You're not your brother, and I cannot keep looking at you as if you are. It'll take me a little bit of time, but we'll work through it all together." When she finished speaking, she stepped up to me, placed her hand on my chest, and rose to her tiptoes so she could kiss me on the cheek.

She was gone all too quickly, giving Cassiel and I space to talk. But the warmth from her kiss and the warmth it brought on lingered. I brought my hand to my face, touching the spot as it faded ever so slowly.

"There's something special about her, isn't there?" Cassiel asked, pulling me from my thoughts.

"Yeah. There sure is," I whispered.

Coming closer, he cupped my neck. "What's going on, Mare?"

"I just miss Sameera."

"There's something else. I can feel it through our bond."

I sighed, "I just got a little jealous watching you and Anevae, but I'm fine now."

His eyes glowed as he brought his hands to my cheeks, forcing me to look at him. "Why are you jealous?"

"Cassie, let's do this later, please."

"Don't fight with me about this. *Please*. We're mated to each other and you're safe with me. I never in my wildest dreams imagined I could mate with or love anyone the way I'm prepared to love you. Please tell me what's going on inside that gorgeous head of yours—why you're jealous of a woman we'll likely be sharing," he whispered as he stroked my cheeks.

"I was raised to believe that we only had one fated mate, and if we found them, we were incredibly lucky. Now, I have two. Sameera is far away and has been for years, and you... Well, I'm not even the one you *want* to be mated to—it just happened. What really hurt was that the first thing you told me was you wished Anevae was your first. Then, you whisked us away to her room.

"I've spent the better part of my life I haven't been anyone's first choice, especially when it came to my father. The only one who's made me feel like I'm important is Sameera. When you guys first told me about the prophecy, I was skeptical because I'm not special enough for something so ground-breaking. But gods, did I want to believe it. So I went to your room this evening, hoping to help you and clear the air a little. Instead, I've muddled things up, and I'm jealous because she was the first thought on your mind when you'd just claimed me as yours. That's a me problem though. I'm new to this and just trying to acclimate myself."

His sadness and remorse immediately washed through our bond. "I-I'm sorry. I've been so focused on Anevae since I made the connection between her and the prophecy that I didn't take the time to consider how everything I was doing would make you feel. What a fucking stellar impression I'm making. We're all part of this prophecy and I care for you deeply already, Amareon. This is all new to me, too, and I'm trying to find my way through things, but that doesn't excuse my behavior."

"Thank you. At least with such a large group things will be interesting. Especially because some of us haven't shared partners before, it'll be a big work in progress, but we'll get there." Then, I looked him in the eyes and waggled my eyebrows. "The group sex is likely going to be fun."

Cassiel shook his head before leaning in and brushing his lips against mine. "I hope you thinking about group sex means you forgive me for making an ass out of myself. Or do you need me to get on my knees and grovel for your forgiveness? Because I will."

With a light chuckle, I stepped forward until we were flush with each other and wrapped my arms around his midsection. "Maybe you can grovel a little later. Let's go fill in the other two about what's happened."

Cassiel and I sat on the couch opposite Anevae and Emrhys, who were cuddled up next to each other, waiting patiently for us. I was nervous about telling them what happened in Cassiel's bedroom. It wasn't that I was ashamed, I just didn't want them to judge me.

Anevae was the first to speak. "What did you guys come to tell us?"

Beside her, Emrhys' eyes focused back on me, pinning me with a severe look. I glared daggers at him, stressing for him to keep his mouth shut about what he'd seen. He was really going to piss me off if he wasn't careful, which sounded like the status quo for him.

Cassiel squeezed my hand. "Amareon and I accidentally mated."

Anevae's eyes grew to the size of saucers as she leaned forward. "How?"

Cassiel started from the beginning, explaining the scent bombing and how things got heated. I was grateful that he skimmed over the part where I was on my knees with his cock down my throat because I had a feeling Emrhys would've had something snarky or extremely inappropriate to say about that. Then, Cassiel explained the kiss that followed and turned around to display the leaf on the back of his neck—my mating mark.

"So that's how fae mark their mates? Does the mark have to do with their magic?" Anevae asked.

I nodded. "Sameera has that exact same symbol on her chest where I marked her. I have plant magic."

Her brow furrowed. "That makes sense. But how do you know the bond is completed?"

Standing, I pulled off my shirt and faced my side toward where Anevae and Emrhys sat. Anevae stood, coming to inspect my exposed skin. She traced her fingers around the golden outline of Cassiel's handprint, and goosebumps spread across my flesh. Inside the handprint appeared to be a word written in the ancient language, but I couldn't read it from my point of view. When she made it all the way around, she looked back at Cassiel, mouth open in awe.

After several moments, she took a step back, and I took that as my opportunity to sit back down. She looked between Cassiel and me before asking, "Do either of you know what this word means?"

Cassiel shook his head. "It's in the ancient language, so that's Amareon's expertise, not mine."

Her gaze turned to me, and I said. "I can't see it well enough from this angle."

"Damn it. Where is my phone when I need it?" she hissed.

Cassiel and I looked at her with questioning glances while Emrhys threw his head back and laughed deeply. Anevae pinned him with a narrow-eyed glance, and he stopped, throwing up his hands. "It's just funny because neither the angel nor pretty boy here knows what you're talking about."

Anevae rolled her eyes. "No shit, Sherlock. But you need to keep it down. You're being really fucking loud and it's late. Hopefully, Aeros isn't nearby."

Emrhys snorted. "He already suspects we're fucking. I haven't confirmed his suspicion, but dragons don't miss a damn thing."

Whirling on him, she stomped to where he sat. "Fucking seriously? And you didn't think we needed to be more careful around him? What if he reports his 'suspicions' to my grandfather? Just remember, you won't have the same mercy that Maeyve had. He will *end you*, Emrhys!"

The vampire's fury surged, and his eyes glowed a bright red as he rose to his feet and took her face in his hands. "I know *exactly* what I am getting myself into, princess. I would risk my life over and over for you because I fucking love you. Luckily for us, Aeros won't go to your grandfather."

"What makes you so fucking certain?" Anevae hissed, her eyes beginning to glow with a yellow ring around the iris and electricity crackling around her hands.

"Because I have a one-up on him."

"What's that supposed to mean?" she asked.

"I know something that will get him in just as much trouble if I tell the king."

Anevae rolled her eyes. "Enlighten me if you would, *please.*"

Emrhys' lips split into a cat-like grin. "Not only is he ass over tits in love with your sister, but they're most definitely fucking and possibly already mated as well."

"Are you sure?" Anevae asked with furrowed brows, pulling herself from Emrhys' grip.

"I've been a guard for longer than you've been alive, princess. Let's just say I'm always aware of my surroundings and can hear across the hall without problem. He's not being anywhere near as careful as we are. I wouldn't expect anything less from someone as young and arrogant as him, though."

"And just how old is he?" Anevae asked, eyes narrowed on the vampire again.

"I don't think he's a day over fifty," Emrhys said.

Furrowing my brows, I snapped, "Fifty years isn't that young. Anevae and Eirian are young. They're *barely* of age."

"Hey!" Anevae hissed. "I'm in my *late* twenties, thank you very much. I've had time to mature." All three of us men in the room laughed heartily and Anevae's eyes turned to slits. "What the fuck is so funny about that?"

Being the youngest in the room aside from her, I spoke up. "In the eyes of these two," I said, pointing at Emrhys and Cassiel, "you're a baby. I'm almost twice your age—about the same age as Aeros, it seems—and I still have so damn much to learn."

Emrhys threw his hand out at me. "Exactly! He may not be *that* young, but he's not as experienced as some of us. Anyway," he said, dragging the word out. "That's beside the point right now. We got way off track. I know we don't have phones—or cameras really—around here, but Cassiel should be able to send the image to Amareon through their bond."

Cassiel's eyebrow rose. "You say this like I know what you're talking about."

Emrhys groaned. "Oh, for fuck's sake. Just... look at the mark and internally focus on your bond with Amareon. It should send that image across. You guys should also be able to speak with each other through it."

Cassiel looked at me, a question in his eyes. I found the one part of my mind that felt soft and comforting like him and said, *Can you hear me, Cassie?*

The angel jumped, eyes wide. "Was that..."

Through the bond, I laughed. *Yes, you're hearing my voice in your mind. Focus on where you feel our mate bond and try to tell me something.*

Keeping his gaze on mine, his voice quietly came through, *This is really strange. I've never heard about this until now, and I've done so much research on fated mates.*

And where did you do all this research? Baeruil? Because I'm sure they don't know everything there is to know, even though the angels tend to think they do, I said with a smirk playing on the corner of my lips.

His eyes narrowed on me. *That's a common misconception.*

Uh-huh. Sure. Are we going to do this thing or not?

Cassiel nodded, and I stood from the couch. Then, with a deep breath, I turned so my side was facing him. Shortly after, an image of the mark from his point of view popped into my head. Trying to look it over, I closed my eyes so it could come into view a little better.

I stood like that for a moment, mesmerized by the detail, before I shifted my attention to the word in the center. It was definitely in the ancient language, but I was having a hard time reading it clearly.

Can you get a little closer, please?

It took my mind a few seconds to receive the closer image. My knowledge of the ancient language was a tad rusty, but this word was one that I'd heard before—Valaryn. It was used during traditional fated mate ceremonies because of its meaning: the binding of destined souls.

Chapter Fifteen

Sameera

After Maeyve's initial interaction with Moranna, she seemed more determined than ever to take care of the madam, which scared the shit out of me. Madam Tanith wasn't someone I wanted to fuck with, so I tried to stay out of her way at all costs. I'd witnessed firsthand how cruel she could be when she wanted to ruin someone, and I didn't want to be on the receiving end of it. Ever.

Maeyve faking her death and escaping all those years ago meant that she bared the brunt of the madam's rage. And the madam wasn't about to relinquish any of the control she had over my little vixen.

When Madam Tanith first announced Maeyve was returning, rumors circulated amongst the girls in the brothel, speculating how Maeyve got away with her plan in the first place. Everyone knew Madam Tanith wasn't someone you could escape easily; she always had her eyes on us. But Maeyve was given special privileges to travel past the edge of town. Even with the madam's eyes outside the brothel, Maeyve could make connections with others.

Whatever the case, Madam Tanith made it clear she wasn't about to let Maeyve go again. The leash she kept on her wasn't likely to be loosened anytime soon, so we'd have to work with the length the madam was willing to give.

Every night, Maeyve returned to our room after seeing clients more battered and bruised than before. Madam Tanith had begun to take extreme measures to break her, but Maeyve was constantly putting on a brave front in front of everyone. For hours after seeing my last client, I tended to her wounded body and soul. Afterward, we would fall asleep clinging to each other, and she'd unintentionally wake me in the middle of the night, whimpering and crying in her sleep. Without waking her, I'd pull her into me and stroke her hair, all the while whispering reassurances to her.

Seeing how everything Madam Tanith threw at Maeyve affected her, a deep-down piece of me awakened that wanted to fight and get both of us out. Even though Maeyve and I hadn't completed our bond, I still wanted to protect the strong woman sent to give me hope. Between her and the others waiting at the castle, I discovered a purpose I never thought I'd have—somewhere I belonged. And by the gods, did I want everything to fall into place for selfish reasons. So, instead of standing by like I'd been doing for the better part of my life, I was ready to take action; I just didn't know how yet.

Since Maeyve was more comfortable with her mom again, we began spending time with her during breakfast and dinner. It overjoyed Moranna to have her daughter back in her life, and I didn't have the heart to tell her Maeyve's kindness wouldn't last long, nor would it continue once we all left the brothel behind.

Even Marcelene and Mordecai warmed up to Maeyve easily, loving having her around. It was as if they could sense the blood they shared with her. Seeing her interact with them warmed my broken little heart and had me wondering how she would be as a mother. It wasn't like I could give her children, but a girl could dream, right? Especially because I was quickly falling in love with her and wanted to give her the world, or do everything in my power to make sure she got it.

"What's going on in that mind of yours? You've barely touched your breakfast." Maeyve said quietly, holding Mordecai while at breakfast one morning.

Lifting my gaze from my plate, I gave her a small smile. "I'm just thinking."

Her brow rose, waiting for me to give her more information. When I didn't, she prodded me for more. "About what?"

I shook my head and returned to my food, whispering, "Just our lives," before shoving a forkful of eggs into my mouth.

"What about them?" she asked, placing her free hand on my leg.

"It's not something I'd like to discuss here."

"Well, my first client is in about an hour, which should give us some time to talk. When is yours?"

After another forkful of eggs, I said, "Last I checked, I'm open most of the morning. We know that can change at the drop of a hat, though."

"Okay. Well, finish up and we'll head upstairs."

With a nod, I focused on my food while Maeyve played a little more with Mordecai. She was so good with him and Marcelene, and her tension seemed to ease just a bit whenever she played with the kids.

Once I was finished, I took care of all the dishes and returned to our table. She'd already handed Mordecai back to Moranna, but the poor babe was reaching for Maeyve, wanting to be with his sister. My heart grew about five sizes seeing the love he had for her.

Moranna distracted him and shooed us off. "From what it sounds like, you have some things to discuss. Go while you have the chance."

Maeyve and I whispered our thanks and hurried upstairs. When we were safely in our room, Maeyve began pulling out clothes for us. Madam Tanith insisted on a uniform, and though our curves were vastly different, we wore the same size. To most of us, it would've made more sense for her to dress us all differently and accentuate our specific features, but the madam didn't care about that and just wanted to show as much skin as possible.

I threw myself on my bed, settling on my back, and letting out a long breath before I closed my eyes momentarily. The bed dipped as Maeyve climbed up beside me. But then she straddled me and settled her weight on my hips.

My eyes flew open, and I asked, "What are you doing?"

"I'm making sure you can't run off before you tell me what's going on inside that pretty, chaotic head."

Scoffing, I tried to buck her off my hips, but she wouldn't budge. "You don't have to climb on top of me to get it out of me."

She gave me an expectant look without moving. "Then tell me please. It's just us here."

My nostrils flared. "I've been thinking a lot about how badly we need to get out of here, not just for us but for the others, too. Seeing the way the madam treats you, I've finally realized just how fucking bad things are getting and I think it's only going to get worse."

"We're working on it. What else are you thinking about?"

"Sometimes, when I'm seeking a distraction from everything going on here, I think about my future and everything I still want—even though I'm young, I haven't lived a normal life, and often wonder what it would be like. Today, while I watched you play with Mordecai, I envisioned how you'd be with your own child. Because despite your limited experience with children, your brother and sister love you, and you do so well with them. And as if that wasn't enough, I've discovered something that makes me so damn scared." Letting out a sigh, a tear rolled down my cheek. "I-I'm starting to fall in love with you, and it's a slippery slope that I'm flying down with no way to stop myself."

Maeyve's eyes filled with tears as she stared down at me. When she tried to talk, she had to clear her throat of the emotion clogging it. "I'm sorry. Your concern for me is sweet. When you started acting different this morning, I had to make sure you were okay because you weren't the same Sameera I've come to know and have also begun falling in love with."

A tear fell down her cheek, and I reached up to wipe it from her face. She nuzzled into my hand, and the contact provided the comfort I'd been missing since Cahir took me from Amareon.

Unable to stop myself, I pulled her face down to mine, capturing her lips in a passionate kiss. Her hands landed on either side of me in an attempt not to smother me, but I was too lost in the kiss to care. Snaking one of my hands around her neck, I buried it in her hair to pull her flush against me and deepen our kiss.

A moan escaped her, and every thread of self-control I had snapped. My succubus took over, the familiar heat spreading through my body as my core throbbed harder than ever. I bucked my hips, grinding my pubic bone against Maeyve's pussy. Her mouth fell open, and I bit down on her lip hard enough that I punctured the skin. When I released it, I lapped up the sweet blood before the wound healed itself.

Easing my grip on her, I let her push herself up for a moment and said, "If your blood tastes that sweet, I can't imagine how good your pussy tastes." Her orange eyes bore into mine, and I licked my lips, rolling the bottom one between my teeth. Then, without warning, I flipped her on her back. "I think I'd like a little taste. You need to get undressed shortly, anyway. Maybe I can make you feel good before you have to face the madam's fucked up clients for the day."

I didn't give her a chance to respond before I began trailing kisses down her body, removing her clothes piece by piece as I went. When I pulled her shirt over her head, her perky tits bobbed with each breath she took. Palming her breasts, I brought my mouth down to suckle on one of her nipples. I licked around the stiff peak several times before I felt her succubus awaken, sending a new, more intense rush of warmth straight to my core. My grip on her breasts tightened, and she sucked in a pained breath. I didn't let that fool me, though, because moments after, the scent of her sweet arousal filled my nostrils.

Letting out a groan, I popped off her breast and helped relieve her of the rest of her clothes. When I looked up, her eyes were already on me, glowing the most beautiful fluorescent orange I'd ever seen. I flashed her a slight smirk before planting more kisses on her belly.

Once she was fully undressed, I shifted my body down and playfully bit her thighs several times. She threw her head back and gripped the sheets tightly. I loved how responsive she was to my touch. Skimming my fingers up the inside of her thigh, she moaned, and I continued until I reached her soaking wet center. I slid two fingers up and down her slit playfully, teasing her long enough that she impatiently bucked her hips.

"You're so fucking wet," I whispered as I brought my fingers to my lips, sucking the tips of them into my mouth so I could taste her. Humming my appreciation at how delicious she was, all I could think about was diving between those sweet thighs and devouring her until the end of my days.

"I need more," she whimpered.

"Such a good girl telling me you need more. But what do you need more of?" I asked, bringing myself so I hovered just centimeters from her lips again.

"Meera, I'm on fire. Please," she begged and attempted to kiss me again.

I sat back up and tsked at her. "*Tell* me what you need and how you want me to give it to you, my little vixen."

Sitting up, she reached for me, and I pulled back just in time. The intensity of her eyes shifted, and she lunged at me. I was nowhere near fast enough for her. When her arms wrapped around me, I squealed, and she straddled me again, pinning me to the bed. In an instant, she had both of my hands above my head, with a sly grin.

She brushed her lips against mine and moved to my ear. "Do you know what I want?"

"No," I whispered breathlessly and swallowed before continuing, "but I have a feeling you're finally going to tell me."

Kissing the sensitive spot below my earlobe, she huffed out a laugh. "You'd be correct. But now I'm going to make you wait longer."

I let out an exasperated sigh. "You were just—"

Pleasure shot through my body, stopping me mid-sentence and stealing all the air from my lungs when she bit down on my neck.

My core flooded with even more heat and wetness, preparing me for whatever was on her mind.

"Fuck, Maeyve."

"That's what I intend to do... Fuck you, that is," she said, making quick work of undressing me.

Thanks to the overwhelming lust fueling Maeyve's actions, she ruined most of my clothes in the process of undressing me, but I didn't care. When we finally escaped the brothel, I wasn't taking the clothes from the worst years of my life; I was going to have a fresh start.

Once I was naked, she placed one hand on my wrists and ran the fingers of her other hand across my bare skin, leaving a trail of goosebumps behind. Her fingers stopped when she reached my knees. Biting her lip, she brushed the tips across the soft skin of my inner thigh, heading directly to my throbbing core.

Her fingers moved at a tortuously slow pace as she spread my folds, running the tips of them up and down my soaking wet flesh before stopping at my clit. She circled it several times, and my breathing increased tenfold, wanting *more* from her. I wanted her to consume me alive and leave me in a blubbering mess on my bed.

The pressure on my clit eased up, and she removed her fingers, coated in my arousal, from my center. I immediately missed her touch. When I began to whine, she brought her fingers to my lips, smearing my arousal across them. Then she parted my lips and shoved her fingers in with a silent demand to clean them off. I obeyed without question.

As she watched me, she brought herself closer. Pushing my luck, I added a moan or two to see her reaction. To my amusement, her nostrils flared and her eyes darkened to such an intensity that most people would've run in fear if they'd seen them like that. But I wasn't like most people. Instead, I met her gaze as she leisurely slid her fingers from my mouth.

"So fucking beautiful," she whispered just before bringing her lips to mine in a sensual kiss.

I pulled at my hands, wanting to wrap her in my arms and keep her close. But she clamped her hand around my throat and sat up. "And so damn impatient. We're going to have to break you of that."

Rolling my eyes, I said, "We both know you're no better than me. You acted the same way when I was the one on top of you. This all has to do with control. With women, I always try to top from the bottom, and it seems you do too."

"You might be right. Or maybe I just want the person on top to give me what I want, and they're not doing it fast enough."

"That sounds like topping from the bottom to me," I sassed.

She moved as quickly as lightning, swooping in and biting my neck playfully. I bucked my hips, grinding against her pussy with a loud moan. Her delicious form of torture had me on the brink of losing my ever-loving mind with lust. Which had never, *ever* happened to me. I couldn't help but wonder if it was the bond begging to be completed.

Maeyve's hand tightened around my throat before she rose to look me in the eye again. "Gods, what are you doing to me, you little demon?"

The corner of my lips tipped up in a smirk, and she shook her head. Her grip on my throat loosened as she moved one of her legs to sit on the outside of my hip and shifted me partly onto my side. When her pussy met mine, I knew exactly what she was doing.

"Now we can both control things. Roll those hips for me. Make us both come," she demanded.

We each rolled our hips, trying to find a good rhythm, and it didn't take us long. The pressure on my clit paired with the lust already flowing through my body was enough to have me combusting in no time. She followed me over the edge, and I took advantage of her distraction to shove her on her back so I could taste her sweetness again. I lapped up her arousal like I'd never taste her again.

"Oh, gods, Meera. I'm so fucking sensitive," she whimpered.

"You just taste so damn sweet."

"Meera, please stop. Fuck. *Please.*"

Pulling back, I placed a kiss against her thigh and then bit her hard enough that my teeth punctured her skin and began the mating process with her. Her blood hit my tongue just as another orgasm hit her hard and fast. I grabbed her thigh, not wanting to soak our sheets in blood, and pulled my teeth from her skin so I could seal the wound.

When Maeyve caught her breath, she shoved herself up. "Meera, what the hell? That wasn't a great idea."

Shrugging my shoulders, I wiped my mouth and rose to my knees. "It was going to happen, eventually. My bond was aching for you, and I'm not willing to fight it anymore. I fucking want you. And I want you to be mine in every single way. Let me agonize over it being incomplete if you don't feel the same way."

Maeyve growled. "Of course, I don't want you to fucking *agonize*. I just hope the madam doesn't see my mark, because if she does, I'm not sure what will happen."

"We'll cross that bridge when we get there," I said through gritted teeth.

Maeyve lunged at me and had me on my back again. Then she latched onto my breast and bit down so hard I was screaming. Fire spread through my veins, quickly turning to such an overwhelming pleasure that I was exploding beneath her again.

That was the last thing I remembered before I passed out.

Chapter Sixteen

Maeyve

When I bit Sameera and realized she'd gone slack, I immediately dug my fingers into her neck to check for a pulse. Relief flooded through me when the steady thrum of her beating heart bounced below my fingers. While my worry lessened, I was still slightly concerned about why she'd passed out in the first place. I made a mental note to ask her about it later.

Looking down at her, frustration settled in. *Why is it that both of the women I'm mated to seem not to think things through all the way?*

Excuse me? Anevae asked, irritation lacing her voice.

Shit. That was supposed to remain in my own head, I said as I stood from the bed to get Sameera cleaned up and comfortable.

I kind of figured that was the case. Care to explain?

My cheeks flushed as I retrieved a washcloth and returned to my new mate so I could clean her up. *Sameera initiated our mate bond—on purpose—without discussing it with me first.*

It was going to happen anyway, right?

My frustration turned to anger, and I slowed the movements of the washcloth over Sameera's body. *That's kind of beside the point! There are things we need to consider when it comes to the brothel and the madam. My biggest concern is what would happen if the madam sees our marks. I'm fairly confident she won't kill me, but I'm sure she'll gladly kill Sameera to punish me. Fuck! I need to get us out of here—the sooner the better.*

Let us help you. Please, Anevae begged.

No. I won't bring you into this mess. Madam Tanith is doing everything in her power to break me, and I will not *risk anyone's life.*

Emrhys finally had enough and chimed in, *And how exactly do you plan to best her? I can still feel how damn weak you are. You won't be able to face her without help.*

You know what? Fuck off, Emrhys. I'm not that fucking weak. And I have Sameera, I said with a growl.

His laugh reverberated through my mind, which only served to piss me off more. *Should we have pretty boy ask her how you're holding up?*

I rolled my eyes, knowing he was talking about Amareon. He was always quick to hand out nicknames. *She's sleeping right now, so he won't be able to talk to her at the moment.*

You're telling me that between the time we felt the shift in your bond—our bond with you—and now, she fell asleep? I'm calling your bluff and asking Amareon to contact her. Unless you have something you'd like to tell us, Anevae said.

My gaze shifted to my new mate. I had no clue how I'd tell them she passed out without them freaking out, so I chose not to answer Anevae and watched Sameera's chest rise and fall with each breath she took.

She isn't answering him, but something isn't right. I don't know anyone who falls asleep right after having sex, especially this early in the morning, Anevae said, her tone harsh and accusing.

Trying to put my thoughts together, I brushed a piece of hair from Sameera's face. *She... passed out after I bit her.*

I have way too many visuals running through my mind and not enough of you to satisfy them right now, Anevae said, a shot of lust slipping through our bond from her.

Glad to see we're all horny as fuck again. But we're straying so far from the point of this conversation! Please let us help you, baby, Emrhys said, desperation filling his voice.

My voice was firm when I responded. *No. Now that I have a mate nearby, I'll be able to heal quicker. I just need to figure out the madam's weaknesses, but I don't even know what kind of being she is. If I had to guess, I'd say she's a succubus or some sort of mid-tier demon.*

I'll see what I can find on her, Emrhys said.

Em, please be careful. I know she's powerful and not a force to be reckoned with. She has a lot of sway here, I said.

Emrhys' laugh trickled lightly through our bond again, and I missed him more than I wanted to admit—especially that damn laugh. *I've been on missions that are far more dangerous than getting information on an evil madam. I'll let you know what I find no later than tomorrow.*

Sorrow filled our bond, and Anevae's voice came through in barely a whisper. *I hate to cut this conversation short, but we have to get to my lessons, my love. Please keep us updated as much as possible. I love you so much and I miss you greatly.*

My eyes welled with tears. *I love you both so very much. I can't wait to have you both in my arms again. Please stay safe.*

I've got us, babe. You take care of yourself and the sleepy kitten. I love you and we'll be seeing you very soon. Even if I have to break in there and take you myself, Emrhys said jokingly, but I knew he was all too serious about it.

Em, I growled in warning.

You know I'm kidding... Emrhys said, hesitating on the last word, mostly. *Anyway, I have to get ready. I'll talk to you soon.*

I'll be waiting, I said, and then closed off our bond.

After a few deep breaths, I refocused my attention on Sameera, who still hadn't woken up. When she was all cleaned up, I put the washcloth in our hamper and threw on my clothes quickly. It was already almost time for me to meet with my first client. In that moment, I was happy that Sameera and I had bonded because we could communicate with each other at all times, and I could check on her periodically throughout the day.

As I put on my skirt, I glanced down at the mate mark on my thigh. Its placement was highly inconvenient for my line of work—everyone would see it. I just had to hope that none of my clients would report it to the madam.

Once dressed, I lay on the bed beside Sameera, who was still fast asleep. Placing my hand on her cheek, I tapped into our new bond to check on her. More than anything, she just felt really tired. I doubted my calming ability would help, but I sent her a little jolt to see if that would allow her to fall into a deeper sleep for the time being.

I lay there for a few more minutes, admiring her beautiful features while she slept, before I had to get up. Leaving her vulnerable and without my protection felt wrong, but I had no other choice unless I wanted to face the wrath of the madam, so I placed a kiss on her forehead and pulled the blanket up over her body.

Sameera's frantic voice echoed through our bond in the middle of my session. *Why didn't you wake me up before you left?*

Trying to keep my face stoic, I said, *Because you were tired after our escapades. You needed some rest.*

I have a client!

Meera, I planned to check on you after the client I'm with. You still have well over an hour before your first client.

We had a walk-in, she hissed. *One of the other girls had to wake me up, and now I'm scrambling.*

Shit. I didn't really think about that. I'm sorry.

It's fine. I'll see you in a bit, she said, before severing our connection.

My blood boiled, and I forced the bond back open, ignoring the man pounding into me. *Do* not *do that to me. I don't deserve your attitude. I was just trying to take care of you. Please tell me if anyone acts weird today.*

The majority of our clients act fucking weird. Now, pay attention to your client before he takes offense. Good. Bye, she said, punctuating the last two words heavily before forcing our connection shut again.

I grounded myself and refocused on my client, funneling my succubus magic into him again. After two more pumps, he was finally done. Without a word, he withdrew from me and left the room shortly after.

When it was time for lunch, I entered the kitchen to find Sameera sitting with my mom and the kids. I rushed to grab some food before joining them.

The first person I greeted was my little sister, sitting at the table doing some homework with her empty plate shoved to the side. "What are you learning about today, sweet girl?"

"We just started learning about demons today," she said, not even looking up at me from her papers.

Lowering my head next to hers, I whispered, "Did you know that you and I are both part demon?"

Her eyes shot to mine, and my mom glared at me.

"I'm part demon?" my sister shrieked.

With a nod, I said, "You sure are. We're both succubi because our fathers were incubi—"

"Maeyve," my mom growled.

"She deserves to know what she is and what she'll be able to do in the next few years. Not to mention, you didn't stop me from knowing at her age," I said, eyes narrowing on my mom.

"Marcelene, we can talk about this another time. Focus on your homework, please," my mom said.

With a sigh, I kissed my sister's head and moved on to greet my little brother. He instantly reached for me, and without hesitation, I put my plate on the table so I could swoop down to take him from my mom. Pulling him in for a tight hug, I asked, "How's my little Cai Guy today?"

"Cai Guy love Maeyveee," he said, throwing his arms around my neck and giving me a sloppy kiss on the cheek.

"And Maeyveee loves her little Cai Guy. Are you being a good boy for mommy? If not, Maeyveee is going to have to give Cai Guy some major tickles!"

"I be good!" he screeched.

"Mom, is Cai Guy being a good boy?" I asked.

With a small chuckle, she said, "Yes, Mordecai is always a very good boy."

"Good," I said, just before kissing Mordecai on the cheek. "Let Maeyveee eat some lunch and then you can hang out with me again for a bit, okay?"

"Otay," Mordecai said with a frown.

After returning my brother to my mom, I grabbed my plate and sat next to Sameera. "How are you feeling, love?"

"I'm fine. Just really fucking tired," she said.

"I'm sorry," I whispered. "Is everything going okay otherwise today?"

"Yeah. You need to eat. I can feel just how tired you are."

Shrugging, I took a bite of my sandwich. "I'm fine."

"You're not. Don't push it too far, otherwise you'll use too much energy and end up like me this morning."

"I'll be okay."

Sameera rolled her eyes and crossed her arms over her chest, pushing her breasts closer together. It took everything in me to keep eye contact with her as she said, "There's no point in arguing with you. You're so damn stubborn."

"I think that's one of my best qualities, though," I teased.

"Maybe one of the most irritating ones," she grumbled.

Leaning in, I whispered, "But you still love me."

"Fortunately for you. I mean it, though. Eat. You still have several clients to see, and you'll use a lot of your energy."

"Fine. But only because I love you, too."

My last client was the most brutal, and I thanked my lucky stars that Sameera encouraged me to eat my entire lunch and dinner. If I hadn't, I may have passed out and earned a big 'I told you so.' I certainly wasn't about to tell her she was right.

After he was gone, I cleaned myself up and returned to my bedroom. Sameera was already there, waiting for me. I walked up to her, gave her a quick kiss, and headed for the bathroom so I could clean every last bit of the disgusting men from the day off me.

Just as I was about to step into the shower, Sameera entered the bathroom, already undressed, and looked me over. "I don't want anything other than to help you clean off. You need some rest."

"Thank you," I whispered and stepped into the shower with her hot on my heels.

True to what she'd said, she helped me wash up, making sure to clean every inch of me. My traitorous body had me wanting more when she kissed the mating mark on my neck and the other on my shoulder—the ones from my mates she hadn't met yet. That thought sparked my curiosity about how she and Emrhys would handle each other, especially because they were similar in many ways.

"What's so funny?" Sameera asked quietly.

"I just can't wait to see how you and Emrhys get along. That's going to be a trip."

"He's the vampire, right?" she asked, touching the mark on my shoulder.

Biting my lip, I nodded. "He's a snarky, sometimes cocky, yet funny and protective bastard. But Anevae and I love him nonetheless for it. You two will definitely get on each other's nerves."

Emrhys, as if summoned, was in my head. *Are you talking about me?*

I rolled my eyes. *Sure am. I was just telling Sameera what she might expect from you. You two are a lot alike.*

Are you and Anevae going to be able to manage that? You already had problems when it was just me.

Well, there are more of us now. We can't all be completely different from each other now, can we? I said.

Sameera's movements stopped on my back. "Is one of your mates talking to you?"

Nodding, I said, "It's Emrhys. He told me he'd do some research and talk to me either later today or tomorrow. Apparently, he sensed I was talking about him."

"What is he doing research on?" she asked.

"The madam. I need to find out what kind of being she is so I can figure out her weaknesses."

"Oh. Okay. Let me know what he has to say," she said before continuing to wash my back off.

I think that's the first time I've heard you be silent when I snarked back. What did you find out? I asked Emrhys.

He was silent for a moment more before saying, *You were spot on with the guess that she's a succubus. But there's something else.*

Are you going to tell me? Or do I have to guess?

He still hesitated, and I was getting impatient. Then, finally, he said, *I think she's... your grandmother.*

Anger rippled through me as I reached to shut off the water, and Sameera immediately went on the defense. "What did he say?"

"Do you know where my mother's room is?" I asked, my voice trembling.

"Y-yes. But Maeyve, what did the vampire say about the madam?"

Taking a small breath, I turned to face my newest mate. I cupped her face and said, "I'm going to get dressed, and then I need you to tell me how to get to my mother's room. I have to talk to her. Right. Now."

Sameera's eyes turned severe as she ripped her face from my grip. "I'm going with you."

"No. You *need* to stay here. I need answers from her, and with how close you were, I don't know that she'll give them to me while you're around. She's always been the master of putting on a fucking facade."

My mate's brows furrowed, and her jaw clenched tight. "Fine. But I expect an explanation when you return."

"I'll give you one as soon as I return; I promise."

"Fine," she grumbled. I took the opportunity to gently kiss her before heading into our bedroom.

While I dressed, Sameera came out wrapped in a towel and plopped down on her bed. "The best way to get to your mom's room is to go up one more floor and head all the way down the hall to the end. Her door is the last on the left."

Throwing on my last piece of clothing, I said, "Thank you. I'll be back as soon as possible."

I hauled ass up the stairs to her room, then stopped directly in front of it to take a deep breath and calm my emotions. If I allowed myself to stay furious and began yelling, I'd risk waking up my siblings. They didn't need to hear everything I had to say to our mother, especially Marcelene. She was so close to starting her menstruation. If I didn't get her out of the brothel soon, my *grandmother* would start preparing her for work. The thought made me sick.

Finally, I raised my hand and knocked lightly on the door before me. Footsteps slowly approached before stopping just on the other side.

"It's just me. Let me in, please," I said, knowing she'd recognize my voice.

Several locks were undone before my mother's eyes peeked at me through a crack in the door. "What are you doing here, Maeyve?"

I ignored her question. "Are the kids still awake?"

"No. They—"

I forced my hand through the crack, opening it just enough I could wrap my hand around her throat. Her eyes flew open, and she let go of the door, allowing me to stroll inside. Once I was over the threshold, I slammed her door shut and pinned her up against the wall.

"How long have you known who *she* is?" I demanded.

My hand on her throat made it hard for her to talk, so she shook her head vigorously back and forth, tears flowing freely from her eyes.

"You've finally lost *all* my sympathy, *mother.* If I *ever* find out you aren't taking care of Marcy or Cai the way they fucking deserve, I will take them from you. You're a fucking pathetic excuse of a mother and apparently always have been," I seethed.

Loosening the grip on her throat, I allowed her to speak. "I didn't know who she was when I got here. But when you were born, and she figured out you were her granddaughter, things went south quickly for me. She made it her life's goal to torture me in any way, shape, or form. It hurt the most when she went after you, but she made it very clear that she had great plans for you, and I wasn't to interfere if I valued my life. I didn't think she'd do everything she did because you're her granddaughter, but I was so wrong. I'm so sorry I've put you through all of this, and I wasn't the mother you deserved."

Stepping into her space fully, I growled, "Fuck your pathetic apologies. They aren't good enough. Gods, I wish I could fucking kill you right now. How could you?"

"You won't understand the choices you have to make until you have children of your own. I thought you were safe with her, and I could still be around for you. But I failed."

With a scoff, I stepped back and ran my hand through my hair. "What's his name?"

My mother's brows furrowed. "Wh—"

"My fucking father! What. Is. His. Name?"

Fidgeting with her hands, she said, "His name is... Cahir."

Oh, for fuck's sake! I said to all three of my mates.

Chapter Seventeen

Emrhys

Maeyve's burst of anger had Anevae and me both on edge. I wished I could run to her and help her, but she was too far away. And it would look suspicious for me to go to Western Maiviraea without orders from the king himself.

Baby, please talk to us, I said for the ten millionth time in the last few minutes as I paced.

Amareon began tapping his fingers against the back of the couch, and I shot him a look. I was already having a rough time and didn't need any help.

He leaned forward with his elbows on his knees. "I'm just as anxious as you are about this whole fucking thing. And I can't even talk to the one we're worried about! My mate can tell me how yours feels right now, and that's it. Sameera said Maeyve won't respond to her either. What do you think is taking so long?"

I let out an exasperated sigh. "How the fuck am I supposed to know? She probably went to question her mom. Who knows how many questions she has and what her mom has to say? How long has she been gone?"

Amareon closed his eyes and reached out to Sameera again, but I couldn't stay still. I felt like I needed to be doing *something*. Maeyve's bond wasn't closed off—she'd proved just how good she'd gotten at that recently—which meant she'd heard Anevae and me reach out to her. Why wasn't she at least telling us to wait for a minute or something?

When I turned to continue my pacing, Anevae stopped me. *Em, she's okay. We would know if she wasn't. This is kind of mind-blowing news for her. Come sit back down, please.*

I just wish there was something I could do. She doesn't have to face this alone.

Anevae reached up and brought my face down to hers. *Em, you can't solve every problem. It'll be okay. And she has Sameera there with her. How did you find out Tanith might be her grandmother, anyway?*

That's some top secret information, princess, I teased, leaning down to give her a brief kiss. My mate glowered at my deflection. *We have files on influential beings across the kingdom, and I was lucky enough to find Tanith's. Maeyve's name appeared several times throughout, but in the section we used to document family ties, it said that her only known granddaughter was dead. The age of that granddaughter at the time of documentation matches Maeyve's when she escaped to the human realm.*

Maybe Maeyve hasn't answered because she's talking to her mom, Anevae said hopefully.

A few seconds later, Amareon took a sharp breath, and his wide gaze quickly swiveled to where Anevae and I stood. "Shit is about to get really fucking complicated."

"What the fuck is that supposed to mean?" I asked, my panic rising.

Amareon shook his head. "We need to let Maeyve and Sameera discuss things. This involves them the most."

"Is Maeyve at least okay?" Anevae asked.

"She's fine, but I think she's in shock. Tanith *is*, in fact, her grandmother. We should wait to discuss the rest until I have more details," Amareon said.

Pulling away from Anevae, I began pacing again. I hated waiting, but it was something my mate needed, and I had to respect that. Anevae returned to her perch on the bed and worried her lip ring while she watched me. She clearly didn't enjoy waiting either, but she had the same mindset as me.

When Maeyve's voice resounded in my head, I stopped dead in my tracks. *I need help finding a safe house somewhere in Maiviraea. When I get rid of this bitch, I'm luring my fucking father to us and we're taking him out next.*

I'll get to work on that first thing in the morning. What happened? I asked.

After a beat of silence, Maeyve explained, *I'll spare you some details, but I confronted my mother and she confirmed your suspicions. That's not the worst part, though. It's the fact that I now know who my father is.*

Who is it? I asked.

Maeyve's unease hit me hard. *His name is Cahir. He's the one who killed Sameera's parents and abducted her. Cahir and Tanith are working with the Lady of Kaeuil... Sameera's grandmother.*

Please let us fucking help you! Anevae begged.

I'm sorry, my love. Sameera and I have to take care of this. These are our monsters to face, Maeyve said, her voice barely a whisper in my head.

Don't you fucking dare block me out, Maeyve! Anevae screamed at her through our bond.

But it was too late. The depth of her sorrow was the last thing I felt before Maeyve shut down our bond.

When Anevae turned to me, her eyes were aglow, but not just with the yellow ring I'd become accustomed to; the blue was different—more like Cassiel's teal—and red specks were flecked throughout. "I cannot just stand by and do *nothing*," she growled, voice laced with power.

"It's not like we can just leave the castle," I argued.

"I have fucking glamour magic and I've been working with it a lot recently!"

"I know you have glamour magic, but you're not proficient at it yet! Magic wielding like your mom's takes *years* to achieve, princess," I hissed, trying to keep my cool.

Her eyes narrowed to slits. "Fucking watch me. I am *not* my mother, and I would appreciate it if you *never* compare me to her again."

"I'm stating a fact and using your mother as an example, not comparing you to her. She worked with her teachers for over ten years to develop the skills she has; you've been working with your magic for mere weeks."

"And look at how far my magic has already come in that short amount of time. I've caught on to things quickly and can control my electrokinesis far better than I did when it first emerged. Not to mention, I've transformed the training room into several landscapes at this point, and I've been working with my glamour magic on other things recently," she said, with her arms clenched at her sides.

She wasn't wrong—she'd done every single one of those things—but she'd never practiced glamouring others, at least with me in the room.

To prove her point, she walked over to Amareon and touched his face. "This will just be temporary, but I need to show Em what I've learned."

Amareon nodded, and Anevae pushed her magic through her hands, changing his appearance. I stood there, unable to do anything but watch in amazement as she morphed Amareon's features to look like... me.

When she was done, she turned to me with arms crossed. "It's not perfect, but I can do this, Em. We need to get to that safe house she asked for, so we can be there when she gets out. Or if she needs us to help, we'll be closer. I cannot stand by and wait anymore."

I still couldn't take my eyes off Amareon, looking for the imperfections she claimed there were. But there wasn't anything I could see from where I stood. In passing, no one else could tell it wasn't me.

"Amareon, get Cassiel back in here so we can make a plan," I said breathlessly.

"This is a terrible plan," Cassiel said.

Anevae scowled at him. "If you're that worried about it, maybe you should go back to Baeruil while we save Maeyve and Sameera. I *can't* sit around and wait anymore, so you can either help me or get out of my way."

Cassiel's mouth popped open and his anger surged. "You did not seriously just say that. If you think I would let you do this without me by your side, you are *sorely* mistaken, and you don't know me well. I may be more of a pacifist, but I will do absolutely anything to protect you."

Dropping her gaze to the floor, she whispered, "I'm sorry. That was uncalled for."

Her sorrow called to me from our bond. I knew she didn't mean to upset him, but she wasn't thinking clearly. I pulled her into my arms. "Princess, we understand how you're feeling—I'm feeling it too—but we have to be careful. Your grandfather is going to lose his shit when he finds out you're gone. He'll send guards from across the kingdom to retrieve you. We *have* to have a solid plan before we leave."

"I know. Where is the safe house you're planning to set up for Maeyve?" she asked.

"I was considering one on the western border of Eirvanna and Maiviraea. Why?"

"Cassiel, how far north have you traveled in the past?" she asked.

He thought about it for several long seconds. "I don't believe I've been far enough north to help us. I've been to the Kolathus mountains but never actually been to Maiviraea. The only other place I've been to that I think will be helpful to us is northern Eirvanna."

"I have a feeling the mountains could be pretty difficult. Could you possibly convey all four of us to northern Eirvanna?" Anevae asked with a hopeful look.

"I probably could, but it would be pushing it."

I placed my hand on Anevae's cheek and directed her attention back to me. "If we do this, there are some things I need to tell you about."

Her brows furrowed. "What is it, Em?"

I took a deep breath, concerned about how she'd react. "Many beyond the walls of this castle—and even some within—don't support your grandfather and the manner in which he rules."

"That happens anywhere there's a ruler with very few checks and balances. What does this have to do with the safe house?"

I bit the inside of my cheek, considering the best way to explain things to her. "This safe house is manned by rebels hidden within the guard. Not only that, but I'm not the loyal guard everyone believes me to be."

Her head quirked and her lips pursed as she met my gaze. A flash of hurt appeared in her eyes before she wrapped her arms around my neck. "I know the person you are deep down, and that's what matters most to me right now. You can tell me anything."

A sigh of relief left me as I dropped my forehead to hers. "I'm so sorry I haven't told you until now. I've been trying to keep you out of harm's way. I don't want you involved in this, but I think you're the one who will accomplish what no one else has been able to in the past—removing your grandfather from power."

She gave me a quick kiss and sat down on the couch, gesturing for me to join her. Hesitantly, I sat beside her and glanced at Amareon and Cassiel. Their faces betrayed nothing of what they were feeling.

"Start from the beginning," Anevae said, taking my hand in hers.

"My birth name is Caevryn Emrhys Corvaethen, but I've always tried to go by my middle name—Emrhys—since my father and I share a first name. I'm the only son of Lord Caevryn Sorric and Lady Seliora Vaelisse of Lamatorre; the first in line for the noble title when my father dies; the advocate for the people of Lamatorre; and the general of Lamtorre's section of the rebellion movement. When I joined the guard about eighty years ago, I enlisted as Emrhys Caelthorn, a boy orphaned as a babe with no record of who his parents were. I've worked hard to climb the ranks and prove my worth, making my way to the king's personal guard."

Throughout the entirety of my confession, my focus remained on Anevae, watching as her eyes grew wider. I wanted nothing more than to know what was going through her mind. Would she still trust me after this?

Cassiel and Amareon said, "Wow," breaking my concentration on Anevae.

"Wow, indeed," Anevae whispered. "What were your plans once you got close enough to him?"

"We were gathering information to start with. But then he tasked me to get you from the human realm, and I knew you were different. It made sense when you got to the castle, and our hands touched. Now, because of the prophecy and Maeyve gone, I've been so wrapped up in you that I've hardly checked in. We were aware meet-ups would become complicated with how closely I was stationed to the king, and we knew he was rounding up his family, but they're not aware of everything that's happened with you," I said.

"How quickly can you bring a couple of the rebels in? I'm not sure how long the magic will last, but I could make them look like us. Then, Cassiel and Amareon can leave notes saying they had urgent matters to attend to. It'll buy us some time before they send people after us," she said, formulating a quick but slightly flawed plan.

"The ideas for everyone besides Amareon sound great. His father is still watching over him, and Amareon's absence will be reported to the lord. Princess, do you think you could glamour three guards?"

Anevae shrugged. "The worst I can do is try."

With a nod, I said, "I'll be back soon," and headed for the door.

Since it was so late and no one was around, I ran to the barracks as fast as I could. I had three specific lieutenants I'd worked with over the past few years who would work perfectly for our plan. I approached their doors one by one, requested they get dressed, and meet me downstairs in the strategy room in ten minutes. After telling the last one, I made my way downstairs. As I stepped inside the room, my eyes caught on the general leaning against the table where a map of the kingdom lay rolled out.

"Are we finally doing something, Cae—" he began in his gravelly voice.

"*I* am doing something," I hissed. "And I believe I have asked you not to call me that, Kaius."

"I do apologize, Emrhys. I sensed you within the barracks and was curious about what was happening because you haven't visited us nearly as often since the eldest granddaughter arrived. We've grown concerned about where your allegiances lie."

Invading his space, I bared my fangs at him. "That is none of your fucking business. What is your business is that I'm leaving for a while and things are going to get *very* messy with the king. Also, Luna, Therin, and Rune will not be available for the next week or more. Plan accordingly for their absences."

"This is very unexpected, Your Highness. I'm not sure it's really a good idea to be leaving right now. Where are you even going?"

Looking back at him, I considered how much I should tell him about our plans. When I heard three pairs of footsteps approaching, I decided not to say anything that would implicate him. "I didn't ask you if you thought it was a good idea, and I do not have to explain myself right now. As far as where I'm going, all I'm going to tell you is I'm going to Maiviraea. But we will be back soon enough. That information has to be good enough for you right now."

Kaius nodded. "Understood. Please let us know if we can be of service upon your return."

We stood in silence until the lieutenants joined us and I strode toward the door before they could get comfortable. "I'll be in touch, Kaius. Lieutenants, please come with me."

The walk back to Anevae's room took much longer than when I'd left because the shifter and the fae didn't have super speed. When we reached her door, I cracked it open and said, "It's me and the guards I promised."

"Perfect. Come in. Cassiel went to prepare some things," Anevae said.

Opening the door, I shuffled the other three in and instructed them to sit on the couch opposite Amareon to wait. Then, I walked over to Anevae, who'd changed into some more casual clothes rather than the dresses she'd been wearing since arriving at the castle. She'd also laid some stuff on the bed to prepare for our departure.

"Are you sure about this, princess?" I asked.

Reaching for me, she whispered, "Yes. One hundred percent."

I pulled her close and kissed her forehead lightly. "Should we get started then?"

With a nod, she pulled away from me and approached the guards. "I'm guessing you brought the female to use for myself?"

"You'd be correct. Her name is Luna, and she's a wolf shifter."

Anevae let out a breathy laugh. *How fitting that her name is Luna, and she's a wolf shifter.*

I shook my head and rolled my eyes. *Be nice, sweetheart.*

"Perfect. Now, this one," she said, pointing at Rune, "is supposed to be Amareon?"

"Yes. Rune is a fae and, to Luna's left, is Therin. He's a vampire."

"It's a pleasure to meet you all. Em, why don't you and Amareon get some of your clothes while I work on Luna's glamour?"

I walked over to where Anevae stood and gave her a playful smirk. "So bossy this evening."

Grabbing my shirt, she pulled me in for a kiss, but nipped at my bottom lip instead. "Yes, I am. But you know I'm right. Now, go so I can get to work."

Chapter Eighteen

Anevae

I'd been taking extra time to work on my glamour magic, both in and out of class. I'd mostly been working with inanimate objects, but there'd been a few times when Amareon let me practice on him while Cassiel and Emrhys were discussing something or another. The glamour didn't last long during those practice runs, but with a book I'd found in the library, I'd learned how to make it last longer; I just hoped I wouldn't overdo it.

Sinking to my knees in front of Luna, I pinpointed each feature I'd need to adjust for her to look like me. I started with her hair because it was one of my most identifying features. The long, silky strands of her straight, chocolate brown hair were drawn into a high ponytail, which I'd not worn many times since arriving at the castle.

"I apologize, but I'll have to take your hair down," I said quietly.

Luna gave me a friendly smile. "Do what you need to, Your Highness. I am here to serve you."

Whispering my thanks, I lightly pulled the band from her hair, not wanting to hurt her. Then I slid it onto my wrist and ran my hand through her hair. Taking a deep breath, I closed my eyes and thought about how my hair looked. Once I had the vision, I focused on the light, tingly feel of my glamour magic, and sent a shot of it to my hands. I stayed like that for a few seconds before I opened my eyes to assess my work.

It was so perfect that it took everything in me not to squeal with joy. Pride filled my chest as I moved on, piece by piece, making the woman before me my replica. Emrhys had done well picking her because I barely felt like I'd used any power when I was done.

"The first feature I've changed that will shift back to your own should be your hair. Once that starts to happen, you may need to hide until everything has returned to normal," I explained.

"Understood, Your Highness," she said, voice still her own, and I muttered a curse.

"Forgot about the voice. Look up just slightly so I can glamour that as well." Carefully, I grabbed the part of her throat, just under her jaw, that contained her voice box. I hummed a natural note and sent a shot of magic to my hand again. When it dissipated, I removed my hand. "Can you say something, just so we can make sure it worked, please?"

"How does this sound, Your Highness?" she asked, her voice identical to mine.

"Perfect! Now I need you to head over to my armoire and pick out a gown for tomorrow that you'll be comfortable in. Anytime you're seen outside this room while glamoured as me, you'll *need* to dress and attempt to walk like me."

She nodded and walked to my armoire while I looked between the other two sitting on my couch. Both Emrhys and Amareon were important to glamour, but Emrhys would be the most important to replicate. Therin's hair was already similar to Emrhys', but other than that, they looked nothing alike.

Just as I was about to start on Therin's glamour, Emrhys strolled back in. "Gods, you have perfect timing, Em. Will you come sit next to Therin, please? Glamouring him will go quicker if I have you here for reference."

"Of course, princess. You did pretty well with Amareon earlier, though," he said as he threw his things on the bed and approached me.

"Well, you were in the room, and I'd just been looking at you. But I've also glamoured Amareon a few times before this," I admitted.

Emrhys sat in the empty spot on the couch and reached for my hand, placing a quick kiss on my knuckles. "You're doing wonderfully."

Heat crept across my cheeks as I slipped my hand from his and got back to work. The hardest part about the glamouring for Therin was that Emrhys had a full-blown beard, and Therin was clean-shaven. When I was done, I glanced between the two vampires. I could barely note their differences, and I knew most people wouldn't pay as much attention as I did. I let out a satisfied sigh.

Emrhys' gaze shifted to Therin, and his eyes went wide. "That's creepy as fuck. He looks exactly like me."

I huffed out a laugh and shook my head. "You've seen me make two others look like you today and this one is creepy as fuck, not when I'd adjusted Amarcon's features?"

"Don't get me wrong, Amareon's was startling, but I watched you do his glamour. I didn't look while you did Therin's. It's just fucking wild to me how identical he looks to me."

"Whatever. I wonder what's taking Amareon so long."

Emrhys shrugged, but when I pursed my lips and pinned him with a glare, he closed his eyes to listen for the fae we were missing. "He's coming down the hallway now. I'll go let him in. Therin, just stay here for now." Once he returned with Amareon, he disappeared with Therin to speak with him.

Amareon sauntered into the room with a bag packed and a pair of clothes ready for Rune. "Sorry, I can't move as fast as the vampire. Plus, I haven't spent much time in my room, so it took me a bit to find things."

"That's okay. Can you sit beside Rune, please?" I asked, gesturing to the empty spot on the couch.

"Of course," he said as he walked past me and tossed his things on the empty couch. Then he circled the table and took his seat.

This time was a lot slower because the only thing that was similar from Rune to Amareon was their build and height. Other than that, Rune's dark hair was cut short to his scalp, his lips were too thin, his eyes were a completely different shape, and his nose was way too narrow compared to Amareon's.

The last thing I changed on Rune was his eye colors. I wanted to make sure they were identical to Amareon's—all the way down to the patterns of his irises. Once I finished, I sat back and admired my work. For being as tired as I was, I'd actually done a great job with the glamour on Rune.

Emrhys came up behind me and kissed the top of my head. "Great job, princess. They all look perfect. I truly hope you can make it stick for a day or two, at the least."

"I think I've got that covered. Why don't you tell them everything they need to know while I gather some of my things?" I suggested, looking back up at him.

"Sounds good. Don't pack too heavy. Remember, Cassiel has to carry me, you, *and* Amareon."

"Yeah, yeah. I'm only bringing my book on glamour magic and an extra pair of clothes. I'm sure we can find somewhere to get anything else we may need."

Emrhys grabbed my chin lightly between his thumb and forefinger, and then said, "Good girl," in that voice that made me want to do dirty things to him. The smirk on his face told me he was well aware of what he was doing to me.

"May I *please* get up... daddy?" I said sweetly, batting my lashes at him.

"Fuck," he growled before leaning down to brush his lips against mine. "That wasn't quite fair, princess."

"You started it with the 'good girl.' Two can easily play that game."

We stayed there, staring at each other, until the energy in the room shifted and Cassiel appeared next to us. Staring down at us, he crossed his arms over his chest. "Is this how you're spending your time when we have plenty of other things we need to be doing?"

Emrhys rolled his eyes, released my chin, and stood to his full height. "Why did you have to convey yourself *directly* next to us? We were in the middle of something. Plus, our girl here has already worked pretty hard. Have a look around the room."

Cassiel's jaw ticked as his eyes drifted from where I still sat. When he spotted Therin, his eyes widened, but then he saw Luna and his jaw dropped. "Wow. You did amazing."

Finally able to stand, I stuck my tongue out at Emrhys and pushed past him to Cassiel. Rising to my tiptoes, I kissed my sweet angel's cheek. "Thank you. I'm particularly proud of my work on Rune. I spent extra time making sure his eyes were just right. But, I must say, I had a pretty great teacher who helped me learn how to focus and harness my magic. I couldn't have made it this far without you."

"Kiss ass," Emrhys whispered and then smacked my ass before he rounded up the guards to talk them through our routines.

I flipped him the bird, and Cassiel chuckled, a sound I rarely ever heard come from his lips. Then he wrapped me up in his arms and kissed me breathless. When he finally put me down, he whispered, "I'm so proud of how far you've come. And I can't wait to see what comes next for us all."

"Me either, but I need to finish packing my bag so we can get out of here as soon as possible. Can you make sure Em tells the guards everything they *need* to know? And how they'll pass off your absence. The glamour I placed on them should last for a couple of days, at least, which means they'll need to keep up our routine as normally as they can until the magic begins to slip. I hope we can make it to the safe house by then."

Cassiel leaned down to kiss my forehead and said, "I can do that. Make sure—"

"Yeah, yeah. Em already told me to pack light."

With a smile, Cassiel's voice dropped to a low timbre as he whispered the same words Emrhys had a minute or two before, making me want to sink to my knees and worship him. Instead, I pushed away, huffing a breath before retreating to my armoire. With each step away, my pussy throbbed.

These damn men, I hissed to myself.

I heard that, princess. When we get to the safe house, I'll show you what 'this damn man' wants to do to you. Maybe we can get Cass and pretty boy to join us, Emrhys' lust-filled voice echoed in my mind. *Your arousal is overwhelming—intoxicating—and I'll never be able to get enough of it. But right now, Luna and Therin can scent you, too. And I want to rip their throats out for even possibly wanting you because you are MINE.*

Continuing to walk toward my armoire, I stifled a groan and tried to push him out of my mind. When he wouldn't retreat, I said, *If you want me to stop being aroused, stop putting thoughts into my head and let me pack my damn bag so we can get out of here.*

Fifteen minutes later, Cassiel conveyed Amareon and me to his bedroom. Emrhys arrived mere seconds later, insistent that Cassiel should save even a small amount of energy for the trip to Western Eirvanna. While I agreed, I knew the possibility we would be spotted running through the halls increased the longer we stayed in Castle Rilvara.

Once Amareon and I were steadily on our feet, Cassiel ushered us all to the map he had laid on his bed. He'd already pinned a spot in northern Eirvanna, fairly close to the Kolathus mountains, which I assumed was the area he'd visited in the past. I let my eyes wander over the map for another moment before refocusing my attention on Cassiel.

Pointing at the pin on the map, he confirmed my assumptions, "This is where I should be able to convey us to. While it's not quite where we want to be, it's the best I can offer in this situation, and it'll get us started at least. Emrhys, where's the safe house?"

Emrhys sidled up next to me and reached all the way across the map to a point where the border of Maiviraea and Eirvanna nearly touched Kaeuil. "Right about here, if memory serves me correctly. I haven't been up that way in several years."

"Are there any towns close to Cassiel's pin?" I asked.

Emrhys nodded. "Probably about ten miles north inside Maiviraea. Why?"

"I think it'd be advantageous for us to commission a carriage. Not only will it keep us out of sight, but we'll also get to the safe house a lot quicker," I said.

"You have a point," Amareon said with hesitation. "But we'll have to be careful not to linger in the cities of Maiviraea for too long."

"Why?" I asked, lifting a brow.

Emrhys placed his hand on my lower back. "You already know that Maiviraea is home to mainly shifters and their sense of smell is incredibly heightened—"

"I wish mine were sometimes," I grumbled under my breath.

"You haven't shifted, so that piece of you may not be awakened quite yet. Even when it is, it may not be as advanced as a purebred shifter. They're the ones we're going to have to be most cautious of because they'll be able to scent your royalty—"

"Oh! I remember Maeyve's cousin, Calli, saying something about that when we came through the portal."

Emrhys' hand stopped its movement, and he went eerily still. "Calli? As in Calliope?"

"Yeah," I said with an inquisitive tone.

"She's a fox shifter, right?" he asked.

I nodded. "She looks strikingly like Maeyve, except her fox form and hair are black and white."

"Interesting," he said, thinking. "If my memory serves right, she's the granddaughter of the Lord and Lady of Eastern Maiviraea."

I gasped. "That would make Maeyve related to them as well, right?"

"If she's related to Calli, it would make sense. Just remember that being nobility doesn't make them good. On the contrary, many of the nobles are the exact opposite," he said, worry creeping into his voice.

"I guess that's true," I said with a sigh.

Emrhys leaned in and kissed my temple. "I know you have firsthand experience with your grandfathers. I wish you didn't."

I crossed my arms over my chest and shrugged. "It is what it is. I don't really care, though. For my entire life, I was led to believe my grandparents were all dead anyway."

Cassiel huffed out a harsh breath and kissed my other temple. "Why does that not surprise me?"

"Because my parents lied to me about nearly everything," I said nonchalantly.

"That doesn't make it any better," Amareon grumbled.

"It doesn't, but that's my reality."

"Well," Emrhys began and reached for my chin to bring my eyes to his, "as your mate, I vow never to let that be your future. I will never lie to you. Ever."

"As do I," Cassiel chimed in.

"Even though we're not mated yet, I vow the same. Lies and deception have plagued so much of your life, and you don't deserve that in the slightest. I know I can't make up for what my brother did to you, but I will do everything in my power to make sure you're always safe and taken care of," Amareon whispered, reaching for my hand.

Warmth and comfort spread up my arm as tears welled in my eyes. I'd gotten so lucky with my mates, and I was getting to the point I wasn't sure if I'd be able to live without any of them ever again.

Cassiel reached up with his thumb, wiping away the tears that threatened to escape. "You deserve to have everything you could ever wish for. That includes a family that isn't full of awful people."

Emrhys wrapped me up in his arms and held me tight. "Please don't cry, princess."

My voice came out in the slightest of whispers when I responded. "You're all so fucking sweet and I love you."

Chapter Nineteen

Cassiel

Anevae finally inhaled deeply and said, "Okay. Let's get back to our plan, shall we?"

"Do either of you have connections in the southern part of Maiviraea that we may be able to tap into?" I asked, looking between Amareon and Emrhys.

Emrhys stroked his beard. "None that I can think of right now."

Amareon took a little longer and shook his head. "I can't think of anyone aside from Sameera. She has some family in Maiviraea, but I'm not sure where they are, and I have no way to contact them."

"Would anyone from the rebellion be able to help us out?" I asked Emrhys.

"I can have word sent to the headquarters in Ceraias. They may send a carriage to meet us at Zylithia—the town about ten miles north of where Cassiel will convey us," he explained to Anevae. "I probably should send word ahead to the safe house to let them know we're inbound within the next several days and that Maeyve and Sameera will be joining us at some point."

"Who do you need to talk to for that to get done? I hope it won't take long. We need to get out of here before people begin to stir in the castle," Anevae said nervously.

Emrhys kissed her temple. "I'm going to make it quick, princess. Don't worry about me. I'll be back before you know it."

"Okay, well, go now," Anevae urged, shooing Emrhys. "We'll try to come up with the next steps while you're gone. Maybe we can find the best cities to stop at on the way. We cannot make the trip all in one go."

"Fine. I'll be *right back,*" Emrhys said as he rushed for the door.

"We'll be here waiting!" Amareon hollered, and I elbowed him in the ribs.

"It's the middle of the night! You're going to wake people up if you don't quiet down," I hissed.

Anevae stifled a laugh, and Amareon rolled his eyes.

"What's so funny?" I asked, genuinely curious.

"You're always so serious," Anevae said with a giggle.

Quirking my head, I asked, "Is there something wrong with that?"

Amareon placed his hand on my shoulder. "No, but you need to loosen up a little sometimes."

My nostrils flared and my lips pursed. "I'll 'loosen up' when we get out of here. Do you realize what will happen if we're caught?"

"I know full well what will happen if we're caught trying to sneak the king's granddaughter out of the castle. But no one would be able to walk in here and see that's what we're planning right now. If someone does walk in here, the three of us will get a slap on the wrist and that's it. Emrhys or the guard who's supposed to be guarding Anevae's room would get the brunt of the punishment," Amareon said.

Emrhys was back about fifteen minutes later. The anxiety that was building with his absence finally dissipated, and I could breathe again.

"What did you guys find?" he asked as he approached us.

"There are a few small towns we could stop at on the direct route, but that route takes us solely through Lord Amaroc's territory. It may be safer to cross back over to Eirvanna a time or two," Amareon said, pointing out the route he suggested.

Anevae huffed. "I've already told Amareon that I don't like his idea. I don't care if Lord Amaroc is my grandfather; he can kiss my ass! The route he suggests will take longer for us to get to the safe house."

Emrhys smoothed his hand over Anevae's back. "Princess, Lord Amaroc has eyes and ears everywhere across southern Maiviraea—well, likely across Maiviraea as a whole because of the sway he holds there. If someone sees you, they may report your presence to him and he'll report that to the king, which will fuck up all our plans."

"Well, I can glamour myself," Anevae argued.

"Have you tried to glamour someone's scent trail yet?" Emrhys asked, eyebrow raised.

"No." She pouted, crossing her arms over her chest.

"Then they'll be able to scent a royal *and* the lord's lineage on you, and that'll raise even more suspicions," Emrhys said, leaning in to kiss her temple. "I know you're frustrated and want to get to the safe house quickly, but we have to be smart about it."

Anevae's jaw ticked as she looked over the map again. "Fine."

"Amareon, do we need to worry about your father that far north in Eirvanna?"

Amareon shook his head. "I highly doubt it. He rarely ever leaves Feraetheam nowadays. And his subjects aren't too fond of him anymore. If they see me, it'll comfort them more."

"Perfect," Emrhys said with a smile. "Are we ready?"

Everyone nodded, and we all dispersed to gather our things. Everything I needed was already laid out on the bed. All I had to do was roll up the map and throw it all in my bag.

Just as I was about to begin, Amareon came up beside me. "Can I help you with anything?"

"Make me stop feeling so gods damned nervous about this whole trip," I said as I reached for the map.

Amareon grabbed my shoulders and turned me toward him. Then he moved his hands to cup my face, and the tingling from our bond spread through my body. "Everything is just fine. We'll be on our way shortly. You've got this. We've *all* got this."

Swallowing past the lump in my throat, I nodded, and his lips met mine in a soft, sensual kiss I didn't think was possible from him. Warmth engulfed my body like never before, but I didn't pull away—couldn't. Instead, I pulled him in as close as I could get him. The kiss was intoxicating, and I didn't want it to stop. When he began trying to pull away from me, I gripped his shirt for dear life.

Cassie, I need you to let me go, please, his voice said in my mind, and I released him, jumping back. It was still so new, and I hadn't gotten used to it.

Amareon's hands fell to his knees, and he panted like he'd just run several miles without stopping. I shoved my things aside on the bed, making room for Amareon, and made him sit.

Are you okay? I asked through our bond, not wanting to alarm Emrhys and Anevae.

He nodded, still panting for breath.

Why are you breathing so heavily?

I used a magical ability I haven't used in a while and have little practice with it. I just need a minute to recuperate; you wouldn't let me go, so I gave too much.

Gave too much what? I asked, brows furrowing.

Energy. I have more than one type of magic, he explained, and my eyes widened. It wasn't common for fae outside the royal family to have more than one type of magic, but it wasn't unheard of.

I don't even remember what your primary magic is, and now you tell me you have two? Did you get one from your mom and the other from your dad? Did Ambrose have the same?.

Amareon shook his head, *Both of my parents have plant magic, so I have no clue where I got this other ability from. And, as far as I know, my brother couldn't do what I can.*

Interesting. Are you feeling better? Anevae and Emrhys are approaching.

"I'm fine," he said, still breathing heavier than normal.

"Are you able to take any of my energy... back?" I asked.

"You're going to need it more than I will right now. Trust me. If I didn't give you that energy, you would've likely felt a million times worse when you convey us than I do now."

I pursed my lips.

"Everything okay over here?" Anevae asked, worry creeping into her voice.

"We're fine. I just got a little dizzy when I went to pick up my bag," Amareon lied.

You need to tell her at some point, at least. Remember what we all promised her, I said.

I'll tell her soon, just not right now, he said.

"Cass, you haven't even packed everything up yet. Do you need some help?" Anevae asked.

"Can you just grab a bag from my armoire, please? I'll roll up the map, and then we can just stuff everything in once you get back," I said.

"Absolutely!" Anevae said and went to retrieve it.

Emrhys stepped in closer to Amareon and me. "That wasn't just you getting dizzy. What was it?"

Amareon crossed his arms. "I used my second magical ability to give Cassiel some of my energy so he doesn't use his up completely, and I gave a little more than my body wanted me to. I'm fucking fine now, so leave it. It'll regenerate quickly."

Emrhys' eyes narrowed on Amareon. He was about to say something else, but Anevae approached with the bag. I took it and began throwing my things into it so we could get going.

I appreciate the extra rush of energy, but I kind of wish you wouldn't have done it, I said to Amareon.

Just wait. Once you see how drained conveying us all has you feeling, you'll be thanking me even more. But after you're fully restored from conveying all of us, you can show me just how much you appreciate it.

My cheeks flushed with heat as I stuffed the last shirt in my pack. *Cocky bastard.*

A cocky bastard you already fucking love and you know it.

Gods, you're a fucking smart ass too, I said, rolling my eyes.

You're stuck with me for the rest of our lives, so you'd better get used to it.

Cinching my bag closed, I turned to where the others sat on the couches. "Okay. This is going to be difficult with the three of you, but we'll make it work. You all have to be touching me—"

"Anywhere?" Amareon asked with a smirk.

"Mare," I growled.

"You and I are going to be a great team when it comes to riling him up," Anevae said with a wide smile to Amareon.

"This is serious. If you lose contact with me at any point during the conveyance, you may not make it to our destination."

Anevae's jaw dropped, and Amareon's face went red.

"Exactly. It's scary, so please take this as seriously as I am because I wouldn't be able to live with myself if something happened to you two," I said.

Emrhys' gaze shot to mine. "What about me? Am I not important too?"

I shrugged. "You're a vampire; you can figure your own shit out. I'm sure you've been all over this kingdom and know everything to be careful of. Anevae is unfamiliar with everything here, especially the threats in the wild, and I'm mated to Amareon. While I'm sure he can take care of himself, if something happens to him, I'm fucked." Emrhys brushed me off, and I continued, "Anyway, I need you all to make sure you don't lose contact with me. It's going to take a few seconds longer for us to get there than you've experienced before, but it should still be pretty quick, nonetheless."

Anevae jumped off the couch and rubbed her hands together. "Alrighty then! Let's get this show on the road."

Never having heard that phrase before, I raised an eyebrow at her as she approached me.

Emrhys scoffed. "It's a phrase from the human realm, Cass. We need to get you caught up with the times, apparently. She's going to be using a lot of those terms. Especially because she grew up there."

"I have a feeling being stuck inside a carriage with you three is going to be real fucking fun," Anevae grumbled.

"It's going to be a ball," Emrhys said, appearing behind Anevae and wrapping his arms around her. "How is this going to work, big guy?"

Amareon looked over the three of us. "What if Anevae stands in front of Cass and wraps her arms around his waist? Then, all three of us guys basically surround her and hold on to each other for dear life."

"That would probably work the best," I said.

Anevae seemed to consider it and nodded. "Let's try it."

Emrhys took her chin in his hand and turned her face toward him, kissing her deeply before letting her go completely. When she got close enough, I leaned down and gave her a quick kiss. She returned it eagerly, wrapping her hands around my neck and melting into my touch. But it was over too quickly.

Never once looking away from me, her hands slowly trailed down my chest to my waist. "I love you, Cassiel."

"I love you, too, Anevae. Make sure you hold on tight, okay?"

With a nod, she wrapped her arms around me and squeezed. Amareon got into position on my right. Emrhys was the last to move, taking up the spot on my left. Once he was comfortable, Amareon reached out to him and they wrapped themselves around Anevae, holding onto each other tightly.

"Last chance to back out," I said.

"I just want to get this over with. Let's go, big guy," Emrhys said before leaning his head down against Anevae's.

Closing my eyes, I focused on the spot I pinpointed on the map. "Hold tight. Three. Two. One..."

Chapter Twenty

Amareon

One moment my feet were flat on the ground, and the next I felt like I was free-falling. I held on as tightly as possible to Cassiel and Emrhys, hoping our staying tightly knit would hold Anevae in place. During the seconds we were in limbo, I tried to keep my breathing even. Anevae wasn't having as much luck, though.

Bringing my mouth to her ear, I whispered, "Deep breaths. We're almost there."

Just as Anevae's breathing evened out, our feet hit the ground, and it took everything in me not to let go yet. I needed confirmation from Cassiel that we could release our hold. But no one moved.

Lifting my gaze, I assessed our surroundings. Behind Cassiel were miles upon miles of vast open fields with the castle barely visible toward the left side of my vision. Behind me, spanning for miles on both sides, was nothing but zyelvris trees. It wasn't exactly where he'd pinpointed on the map, but it was pretty damn close.

Clearing my throat, I said, "Cassie, we're on the ground. Can we let go now? I'm sure Anevae can't breathe at this point."

"Yeah," he whispered breathlessly.

We all released our grip on each other, except Anevae. It appeared her grip had tightened.

"I'm rather fine right here at the moment," she said, her eyes still slammed shut.

A smile spread across Cassiel's face, but he said, "As much as I'd like you to stay here, I need you to let go." Then his voice dropped to a whisper as he said, "Don't tell Amareon, but he was right."

Emrhys began essentially prying Anevae's fingers off Cassiel. "Baby, everything is okay. Cassiel needs to sit or lie down, though."

With a whimper, she released Cassiel and clung right onto Emrhys. He welcomed it and moved away with her in his arms, nodding to me in a silent plea to take care of our angel.

I approached Cassiel just in time for his knees to give way. With a muttered curse, I scooped him up before he could hit the ground.

"Gods, you're massive. I'm glad your wings are hidden right now," I grumbled. "Em, we all need a little bit of rest. Can you find us a good spot?"

Emrhys glanced around for a moment. "I don't know anything about what's inside this forest, but I can look."

"No!" Anevae shrieked, still clinging to Emrhys like her life depended on it.

Leaning down, Emrhys kissed the top of Anevae's head and wrapped her in a tight embrace. "Princess, we can't stay in plain sight. We're still in Eirvanna, and the sun is coming up over the horizon any minute. My skin won't allow me to be in the sunlight for long before I start to develop blisters."

"Do we know what's in the forest?" Anevae asked in a hushed tone.

"No. That's why I planned to look. I'll be in and out quickly. You'll be the first to know about any dangers," Emrhys said, trying to calm her worry.

Reluctantly, she let go of the vampire, and he was gone, darting off into the forest. She stared after him as she swayed side to side. I desperately wanted to comfort her, but having Cassiel in my arms made that pretty difficult.

"It'll be okay. He's going to be right back. Come, stand with Cass and me, sweetheart," I said.

Anevae absentmindedly did as I said, eyes darting all around.

After a few minutes, I shifted Cassiel's weight in my arms and glanced toward the north. A small town became visible in the distance thanks to the rising sun. It wasn't far from the forest's tree line, making my excitement spike. Just as I was about to ask Anevae if she'd heard from Emrhys, his figure came into view, moving at an incredible pace.

There was a scowl on his face, and a nagging concern crept into my mind. "Did he say anything about the town, Anevae?"

"No. Is something wrong?" she asked.

I shrugged, deciding to wait for Emrhys. It took less than thirty seconds before he came to a stop in front of me and beckoned for me to hand over Cassiel.

"Give him here. I found someone affiliated with the rebellion who will let us rest in their inn for as long as we need."

"There's something you're not telling us," I said, holding onto Cassiel tightly.

Emrhys' jaw tensed. "There are guards everywhere in the city right now. The inn is just inside the city limits, but if any of them scent Anevae, they're going to have questions."

I glanced at Anevae and clenched my jaw. "Take her first. Let's get her there before everyone in town is awake. I'll start the walk with Cassie—maybe he'll wake up on the way. Anevae is and always will be the priority here."

"I'll be fine. Give Cass to Em. You and I can start the walk," she said with her nostrils flared wide and her hands clenched at her sides.

Emrhys took a step toward Anevae, but her gaze whipped back to him. "Don't even fucking think about it. Take Cassiel to the inn so he can get some rest while Amareon and I begin the walk to town. I'll be fine. And if I'm not, you'll be the first to know."

"Gods damned stubborn woman," Emrhys growled.

Anevae flung her middle finger up at him. "Get fucking used to it."

Emrhys crowded Anevae's space with one more step and tangled his hand in her hair, yanking her head back so she was looking at him. "I can't wait until I can fuck this attitude right out of you."

I hummed in agreement, unable to stop myself. Anevae's gaze momentarily shot to me before she refocused on Emrhys.

Anevae's throat bobbed. "Let me go so we can all get to this inn and get some rest."

"Are you going to behave?" he asked.

"When do I ever behave?" she asked, biting her lip ring.

Letting go of her hair, Emrhys hissed, "Fine. I'll take Cassiel first, and then we can go from there. When I get to the inn, I'll reach out to see how you guys are doing."

"Thank you," Anevae said, batting her lashes at him.

Emrhys motioned for me to give him Cassiel again. I handed him over hesitantly and muttered, "She's going to be the death of us all, isn't she?"

Emrhys nodded, adjusting Cassiel's weight. "She likely is, but life is better with her in it. She cares about us the way we care about her, and I can't be too upset about that. I just want her to be safe."

I rolled my shoulders to loosen the muscles that'd bunched up from holding Cassiel and whispered, "Get him to the inn. I'll work on getting her there as quickly as I can. If we take too long, come get her, and I'll make my way there alone."

With a nod, Emrhys was off again, and Anevae was stomping off after him, going way faster than she should. Taking long strides, I caught up to her and grabbed her arm to stop her. She whirled around with fire in her beautiful blue depths and ripped her arm from my grasp.

"What?" she asked with a snarl. "We need to get to the inn."

"Yes, we do. But at the rate you're going, you'll wear yourself out before we even get halfway there. Slow down a little bit."

"Fine," she mumbled. Then she turned back around and took off at what seemed to be an even faster pace.

I trailed behind her for several minutes to see how quickly she tired herself out. Amazingly, we made it about a mile before she slowed down little by little. When I caught up to her, I looked her over. Sweat glistened on her forehead and soaked the roots of her hair while her chest rose and fell with shallow, ragged breaths.

But like the stubborn woman she was, she persisted until she couldn't continue and had to stop a few hundred feet later. Bending over, she grasped her knees and tried to slow her breathing. I came to a halt beside her and slipped my hand under her pack so I could rub her back.

"I'm. Fine," she said between pants.

But I knew better. Swinging my pack to my front, I turned around and kneeled on the ground before her. "Hop on. You're not pacing yourself well enough, and I know it's frustrating, so let's try this."

"You're trying to give me a... piggyback ride?" she asked.

One of my eyebrows rose as I looked back at her. "I have absolutely no clue what a 'piggyback ride' is, but I am trying to give you a ride on my back. Maybe later I'll offer you a ride on my front after we rest at the inn."

The scowl plastered on her face was enough to have me busting out in laughter. When I caught my breath again, I said, "Hop on, pup. We're wasting time here."

"For fuck's sake. Not you, too," she grumbled as she approached me. Then, she placed her hands on my shoulders and whispered barely loud enough for me to hear, "Fuck, you're... massive."

The thoughts filtering through my mind had me biting back a laugh. But the flush creeping up my neck had Anevae going on the defense. She shoved away from me and crossed her arms over her chest, pursing her lips and leveling me with a look that told me she was expecting answers.

I rolled my eyes and let out a long breath. "What's wrong now?"

"You were about to start laughing and held it back. Why?"

"I'm not sure you want to know. You're already irritated with me after my *one* comment."

"Well, I guess you heard what I said about you being massive. How did I manage to get more than one of you who's immature?" she asked with an exasperated breath before climbing onto my back.

Once she was situated, I hooked my arms around her legs and stood. "At least you know things will never be dull around us."

"My life is crazy enough as it is."

"While that may be the case, we'll be here to entertain you."

An hour later, we'd finally made it about halfway to the town, and Anevae was fidgeting nonstop.

"You okay back there?" I asked.

"My legs are falling asleep and they hurt like a bitch right now. Can you please let me down for a bit?" she whined.

"Are you going to pace yourself properly? Or are we going to have an incident like earlier?"

"I'll be fine," she hissed through gritted teeth.

"Now, now, pup. Don't cop an attitude with me. I'm asking legitimate questions. If it were up to me, I'd carry you the entire way, but I'm trying to take your wants and needs into consideration." Anevae huffed out a breath against my neck, and I tightened my hold on her legs. "You are *so* getting spanked when we get to the safe house."

Anevae wiggled in my hold. "I need to get down for a while. Please?"

"Are you going to listen to me?"

"Yes," she snapped. "My legs feel like they're going to fall off any second if I don't move from this position."

"Gods, why are you so damn difficult sometimes? You were just being so nice."

"I keep asking you to put me down, but you're not doing it! You'd be getting a little pissy if you were me, too."

I headed for a large tree stump just off the road. "Even though you're not seeing it, I'm trying to do what's best for you. If I let you down and you wear yourself out completely, it'll slow us down that much more. Then, Emrhys will freak out because we're taking too long and he'll insist on coming out here to get you, wearing himself out more than he needs to."

Anevae remained silent until we reached the stump, and she slid off my back. Once she was settled, I stood up and went to take a few steps away when she said, "You're right. I clearly didn't think about all of that. Let me just stretch my legs briefly, and we can keep going."

I took a few steps forward and began stretching my back. "Sounds good. We should make it to the town in the next hour or so. Did Emrhys let you know if he's gotten Cassiel settled?"

"He did, but didn't say much else. None of us has slept in nearly an entire day, so I know he's exhausted."

I nodded. "How are you feeling?"

"I've been better and I've been worse. I just want to get to the inn so we can get some rest. Are you ready? I'll let you set the pace."

"How about you find a comfortable pace for you, and I'll let you know if you need to slow down? My legs are quite a bit longer than yours, so if you leave it up to me, you're likely to get tired a lot faster because you'll be trying to keep up with me."

The corners of Anevae's lips tipped up into a playful half-smile as she met my eyes. "I can do that."

Chapter Twenty-One

Anevae

It took us just under two hours to get to the city limits, and I'd only been able to continue half of the trek on my own two feet. Emrhys wanted to come get me several times when he sensed how tired I was, but I shut him down every single time. He needed rest, and I could handle my own with Amareon, especially since I'd finally convinced myself that he had no intentions of hurting me.

As we finally walked up to the inn, Amareon let me down from his back, and I reached out to Emrhys to let him know we'd arrived. He was outside in an instant, ushering us to the room we'd been given before anyone could start asking questions. His hand rested on the small of my back as we walked, serving as a reminder that he was still there with me and wouldn't let anything happen to me.

When we reached the room, Emrhys opened the door for me. Stepping just over the threshold, my gaze landed on Cassiel, and I stopped in my tracks. He was lying in the middle of a huge bed, sound asleep and stripped to his boxers.

He was a well-sculpted god, and I wanted to worship him every chance I got.

Emrhys stepped around me and playfully swiped at the corner of my mouth before leaning against the table beside me. *You're drooling. Are you going to do that every time you look at one of us when we're not fully clothed?*

I rolled my eyes, threw my bag on the table behind Emrhys, and strolled to the edge of the bed so I could take off my boots. *Have you gotten any sleep?*

He shook his head. *I've been far too worried about you for that. When you lie down, I'll lie down.*

Alright. Will you please help me with these laces? I can't even see straight right now.

Emrhys pushed himself off the table, made quick work of my laces, slipped my boots off, and threw them aside. Then he pulled me to my feet and away from the side of the bed. Another body pressed against my back while two familiar hands wrapped around my middle—Amareon. He buried his nose in my hair, inhaling deeply as his hands found the hem of my shirt and snuck beneath to the soft skin of my belly. Goosebumps covered my arms, and a soft sigh left my lips.

Amareon's hands explored my belly, eliciting more soft sighs from me. Emrhys just stood there, watching Amareon continually caress my body, until he'd had enough and reached for my shirt. He pulled it over my head in a swift movement, leaving only my bra on my upper half.

"I really wish we didn't have to sleep right now. I'd much rather bury my cock deep inside you," Emrhys said, voice husky.

Amareon lifted his head from mine and kissed the exposed skin of my neck. "I rather agree right now. I still have yet to claim you. But the vampire is right—we need to sleep while we have the chance."

"You're both teases," I said, trying to push myself away from them, but Amareon's hands stayed right where they were on my hips, keeping me in place.

"Don't act like you don't like it, pup," Amareon whispered in my ear.

"I'm too tired for you right now," I said, words slurring as a yawn forced my mouth open.

"I know, princess. Let's get you undressed," Emrhys said as he reached for my pants.

I was just about to ask Amareon to fetch my bag when I realized– "Shit. I forgot my pajamas." I sighed and said to Amareon, "Just give me my shirt back.".

Amareon didn't move. "That's not going to be comfortable. Just wear your underwear... Or better yet, wear nothing at all. It'll give all three of us easy access to your cunt when we wake up feeling more refreshed."

Emrhys grinned in agreement as he loosened the last button of my pants, and I glowered at Amareon over my shoulder. "We have more important things to take care of than you getting your dick wet. You're going to need to learn some patience."

He let out a heavy sigh. "If you want your shirt, by all means, you can have it. But you need to get your ass up in that bed and cuddle up with our angel. I'll take his other side, and Emrhys can sleep behind you. You need sleep, pup."

"Fuck it," I mumbled as I climbed into the bed beside Cassiel in just my bra and panties. I was almost asleep the moment my head hit the pillow and barely felt the bed dip when Emrhys and Amareon joined us. Emrhys wrapped me up in his arms, providing me the comfort I desperately needed. Then, Amareon rested his hand on my cheek, and everything felt nearly perfect. But I was still missing Maeyve... and Sameera.

"Sleep, princess," Emrhys whispered in my ear. And for once in the entire time I'd known him, I complied without question.

When I woke, I was flat on my stomach, sprawled across the mattress. None of my three men were anywhere in my immediate sight, and I sat up in a panic. My head whipped around, searching the room for any sign of them.

Everything is fine, princess. Amareon and I went to grab some food for everyone. Cassiel is standing just outside the door. He was worried he'd wake you, Emrhys said calmly, trying to soothe the panic I'd projected to him.

I flopped back on the bed and closed my eyes, trying to calm my breathing. *What time is it?*

About seven or eight in the evening.

Weren't we supposed to be leaving here about midday?

Yes, but you needed your rest, and clearly, so did we, Emrhys explained.

It still fucked up our plans, though. Shit. What about the carriage?

Don't worry about that. I'm securing us a carriage here as we speak, he said with a tone that made it evident there was a smile plastered on his face.

I let out a relieved sigh and Cassiel barged through the door. "Are you okay?"

"Emrhys was just letting me know where everyone..." My words trailed off when I sat up and saw him biting his lip. Hard. His eyes wandered lazily over the swells of my breasts and the bare skin of my belly. Arousal coiled low in my belly, soaking my panties. Skimming my eyes down his frame, they landed on the tent in his trousers. Playing with my lip ring, I asked, "Like what you see?"

His gaze shot back to mine, the teal almost completely taken over by his pupils. "Is that even a question? Of course, I love looking at your exquisite body. Although I'd rather you be completely naked right now so I could see every single inch of it."

"Why don't you close that door behind you and help me get these clothes off, then?"

He took another step into the room and closed the door behind him, but stayed put. "As much as I'd love to take you up on that, we have somewhere we'll need to be soon."

"Aww. No fun. I guess I'd better clean myself up," I said, reaching for the clasps on my bra.

"Anevae," Cassiel growled. "What are you doing?"

"I can't clean up that well when I have all my clothes on, can I?" I asked, glancing at him through my lashes.

Cassiel reached for the doorknob. "Maybe I should just go back in the hallway."

Loosening the last clasp, I slid my bra off. "Or you could help me."

He kept his eyes on mine as his nostrils flared and his grip tightened on the knob. But he still didn't move.

Being the tease I was, I brought myself to my knees and began playing with the hem of my panties. "You want to send Amareon this image to get the other two back here faster? I'm sure they'll have no problem helping me out."

Anevae, Emrhys growled in my head, *what the fuck are you doing to the poor angel?*

I'm offering him some fun before we leave, but he's not taking the bait. Maybe you and Amareon can come back and convince him. It feels like an eternity since I've had Cassiel inside me, I whined.

A few seconds later, Emrhys was trying to shove the door open. "Cass, I kind of need you to move so I can get in there."

Reluctantly, Cassiel took a step forward and released the knob so Emrhys could get in. A sinister smile spread across my lips as I watched Emrhys' face morph into one of pure lust. I loved the effect I had on my men, especially since I'd never been comfortable in my body.

Amareon came barging through the door about thirty seconds later, huffing and puffing. "You guys made me run. This better be fucking... Well, damn. This is even better than I expected."

"I see you didn't get the picture that I suggested Cassiel send you. At least you're seeing it for yourself now," I said, crawling to the end of the bed.

Emrhys cleared his throat and adjusted himself unapologetically before walking toward me. I got back to my knees and licked my lips, ready to face him head-on.

His hand wrapped around my throat, landing directly on my pounding pulse points. "Did you just wake up horny and not tell me, princess? Because right now, you're playing with fire. You can't take all three of us."

"I can take each of you, one right after the other. Or I can take one of you in my mouth and another in my pussy at the same time. Maybe Cassiel can take my pussy, you can take my mouth and Amareon can take Cassiel's ass."

Amareon groaned. "I like that idea. You're going to look fucking perfect coming apart on Cassiel's cock. When you do, I'm going to lick every last drop off of him and devour your pussy whole."

Heat pooled low in my belly, and I rolled my bottom lip between my teeth to keep myself from moaning at the mere thought of what Amareon suggested. He reached around Emrhys and pulled my lip out from between my teeth with his thumb before letting it go. Then, he skimmed his fingertips down my neck and over Emrhys' hand, continuing down to the hem of my panties.

His fingers played with it and the sensitive skin below. "Are you wet for us, pup?"

I nodded enthusiastically, wordlessly inviting him to see for himself. His fingers slid below the fabric, slowly slipping between my folds. He found my clit without a problem and circled it, eliciting small moans from me, before continuing to my opening. He sank two fingers in, pumping them in and out several times.

"Fuck. You're absolutely soaked. Now I need to know if you taste as sweet as you smell."

"Ask Emrhys. He'll tell you," I said, another moan escaping when he curled his fingers, rubbing the sensitive spot high up.

Emrhys' grip on my throat tightened. "Her cunt is fucking delectable."

After pumping in and out a few more times, Amareon withdrew his fingers and brought them to his mouth. He let out an appreciative moan as he licked them clean. "I think I may have a new addiction."

My pussy throbbed, hopeful my men would give me what I wanted. I had no doubts that Amareon would be the first to cave. The way he was looking at me told me everything: he wanted me as badly as I *needed* one of them at that moment.

As I sat there in a silent stare down with Emrhys and Amareon, Cassiel approached the side of the bed. Emrhys released my throat, and I turned my attention to my beautiful angel. His jaw ticked as he looked me over, but he shocked me when his hand shot out and wrapped around my throat. Cassiel was usually so gentle that it wasn't something I expected from him.

He dragged me to him and kissed me hard. When he pulled back, he said, "Gods damn it. Why do you make it so hard for me to be a good man?"

"Because I want you to fuck me. Right. Now. I haven't had you inside me since before Maeyve was taken, and I don't feel like waiting any longer. Don't lie and tell me you don't want me because," I reached down to palm his erection before continuing, "you definitely fucking want me right now. Sometimes you need to let your other head take over."

Amareon walked up behind Cassiel and wrapped his arms around him, undoing his trousers. "Fuck our girl, Cassie. She's practically begging for it."

I stroked Cassiel's hard length over his pants one last time before letting go and allowing the fabric to drop to the floor. Amareon slid his hand under the band of Cassiel's boxers and gripped his cock. Cassiel's mouth fell open on a moan, but Amareon wasn't done; he held onto Cassiel's length tightly as he stroked him from root to tip. Unable to stop himself, Cassiel tightened his grip on my throat.

Watching them was insanely hot, but I needed some stimulation. With my position on the bed, I couldn't rub my thighs together at all, so I slid my hand between my thighs to my clit. I was so focused on the scene unfolding before me that I didn't notice Emrhys crawling on the bed behind me until his arms wrapped around me. Running his hand down my belly, he replaced my hand with his, teasing my clit lightly at first. Then, his fingers slipped further into my throbbing center, finger fucking me roughly. His other hand palmed one of my breasts and pinched my nipple. Moans filled the room, and I wasn't even sure who they were all coming from at that point.

"I need more. Please, Em. Cass. Amareon. Someone please fuck me," I begged, clawing at both Cassiel and Emrhys' hands on me.

Emrhys kissed my neck and nipped at my earlobe. "So demanding today. Are my fingers not enough for your needy cunt?"

"N-no," I whimpered.

Huffing out a laugh, Emrhys slid his fingers from my pussy and I whimpered, desperate for someone's cock. "At least you're honest." Then he ripped my panties off me and spanked my bare ass. The impact stole my breath and amped up my arousal even more. "Cass, I think it's time to give our girl what she wants."

Cassiel nodded and released my throat. Blood rushed back to my head in a whoosh, making me lightheaded. I leaned back against Emrhys to keep myself upright while I looked back at Cassiel's physique. In the time Emrhys had been pleasuring me, Amareon had completely pulled down Cassiel's boxers, so his cock was standing at attention. I licked my lips, watching as he pulled his shirt over his head so he was completely stripped.

Emrhys kissed my cheek and pushed me to sit. Then he scooted back on the bed, nearly to the edge. Shortly after, I heard clothes hitting the floor.

He grabbed my elbow and said, "Turn to face me."

My heart rate increased, but I did as he suggested. I wasn't surprised to find him completely undressed as well, sitting on his haunches with his dick bobbing and begging for my attention.

"You said you wanted my cock in your mouth and that's what I'm going to give you. Cass—you lucky bastard—you get to take her cunt from the back. Spank that sweet ass... It seems she likes that a lot. And Amareon, treat our angel like the bad boy he thinks he's being right now. Fuck that ass so hard he sees stars." Emrhys took complete charge of the room.

More clothes hit the floor, and the bed dipped behind me as Cassiel climbed on. His hands landed on my hips, sending an exquisite jolt through my body. I leaned back into his touch, giving Emrhys the space to ready himself. Looking me directly in my eyes, he stroked up and down his length.

"Are you ready, princess?" he asked, smearing his pre cum over the tip of his cock.

"That's a pretty silly question," I said, returning to my hands and knees. "I'm always ready for your cock, any way you're willing to give it to me, *daddy*."

"Fuck," Emrhys growled, his cock bobbing in his hand. "Why is it so hot when you call me that?"

Shrugging, I dipped down and licked his slit. He sharply inhaled while his cock begged for more. I happily obliged, dropping myself to my elbows so I could take him in my mouth and hiking my ass up in the air for Cassiel. Emrhys' hand released his length and tangled in my hair instead. Cassiel's hands gripped my hips harder, but he still hadn't moved otherwise.

When I took Emrhys deeper in my mouth, he moaned and threw back his head. "Fuck, princess. Your mouth feels so good, but nowhere near as good as your pussy. Cassiel, what the fuck are you waiting for?"

"I-I don't know. I'm just nervous about hurting her. This is all so new to me still," he admitted.

Amareon was the one to soothe his mate's fears. "You'll know if you hurt her; I promise. Dealing with this one and how dominating he can be, I'm sure she can take a lot."

Cassiel stroked his thumbs over my hips before releasing me with one hand and sliding his erection between my folds. I moaned around Emrhys' cock as he tightened his grip on my hair. Cassiel continued sliding himself up and down, hitting my clit with each sweep. My hands gripped the sheets as I whimpered and tried to push back into him.

"So impatient, pup," Amareon said just before a hand came down hard on my ass.

Whimpering again, I jerked forward. Emrhys' cock hit the back of my throat, triggering my gag reflex, and his grip instinctually tightened in my hair, causing tears to well in my eyes. But despite the tears, a wave of arousal flooded through me.

"I'd say she definitely likes to be spanked. She's even more soaked than she was before," Amareon said, plunging two fingers into me.

The pleasure was short-lived, though. When he withdrew his fingers, Cassiel let out a gasp shortly after. My curiosity spiked, and I stopped my pursuit to listen.

"Relax, it'll only sting for a second," Amareon whispered. Cassiel sharply inhaled through his teeth, but then moaned, and Amareon praised him, "Such a good boy, taking my fingers so well. I can't wait to take this tight ass."

Emrhys' cock jerked against my lips, breaking my focus on the men behind me. "Are you having a hard time focusing, princess?"

Taking him back in my mouth, I spoke through our bond, *Maybe a little. I almost wish I could be in two places at once so I could watch them and still take care of you.*

When he hit the back of my mouth, I looked up and watched as he threw his head back, pleasure coursing through his body. His hand, which had loosened its grip, tightened, and my eyes watered again. He wiped away the tear that tried to escape using his other hand.

"Fuck. Cass, take her pussy before I change my damn mind," Emrhys growled.

Amareon chuckled. "You heard him, Cassie. Don't miss out on the opportunity to fuck our girl. I can't wait to lick every bit of her arousal off your cock when she comes all over it."

Cassiel's resolve broke and ran his erection through my folds again and sank into me to the hilt. At the same time, Emrhys thrusted into my mouth, making me gag once more. Cassiel's hand on my hip clamped down hard when my walls constricted around his cock tightly.

"Oh, gods," Cassiel said as he slid out slowly and then thrust in again.

"That's right, fuck her pussy while I finger your tight ass," Amareon whispered to Cassiel.

And Cassiel did just that. He pounded into me over and over, forcing me to take more and more of Emrhys. My moans grew louder with each thrust of his hips.

But then Amareon stopped him. "Cass, pull out of her and move to the side for a moment. I need to get my dick wet so I can fuck you without hurting you too much."

Cassiel hesitated before he slid out of me. I whimpered at his loss, but then Amareon touched my hips and sank into me. He gritted out his own, "Fuck," before pulling out and allowing Cassiel to return to his spot.

When Cassiel thrust into me again, I moaned, but he didn't continue. I bucked my hips in protest, and he spanked me hard. "Patience, sweetheart," he said as he rubbed at the skin.

Impatient as I was, I waited for Cassiel while still sucking Emrhys' cock slowly. My pussy throbbed around Cassiel and, in turn, his cock twitched against my walls. Then, his nails dug into my hips, and he hissed in pain.

I stopped my movements, wanting—no, *needing*—to listen to what was happening behind me. Emrhys didn't urge me to continue, and when I looked up at him, I realized it was because he was nearly as enthralled as I was.

Amareon hissed, "Fucking gods," his voice full of both pain and immense pleasure as Cassiel was forced forward until his hips were flush against my ass. He was hitting me so deep I saw stars, but Amareon wasn't done. When he rocked back, he slammed into Cassiel harder and stayed there for a minute.

Then, Cassiel and Emrhys began moving in a slow rhythm that was going to be the death of me. My grip tightened on the sheets, nearly puncturing them. But it wasn't enough.

Em, I need Cassiel to move faster.

Breath coming in pants, Emrhys said, "Cass, she wants you to go faster. And apparently, I need to remind you I instructed you to smack her ass."

"There's... too much going on right now," Cassiel said, increasing his pace, but not moving his hands.

"I'll take over on that front for you, Cassie," was the only thing I heard from Amareon before his hand came down hard on my ass.

My responding moan and the tightening of my pussy served as an encouragement for all three men to go harder. An orgasm coiled deep in my belly, building quickly, and I was falling apart with a few more thrusts of Cassiel's hips.

Emrhys' restraint snapped. He plowed his cock further back and harder. The second time I gagged, he said, "Breathe through your nose and hollow your cheeks out, princess. Suck my cock like the good girl I know you can be."

I scowled at him, at least the best I could while he was fucking my face, but breathed through my nose as he suggested. Apparently, all he had to do was praise me to get me to do anything he wanted. He pumped his cock in and out of my mouth and his eyes rolled into the back of his head as a moan left his lips.

It was at that moment I knew I was fucked—in more ways than one—and was certain I'd let my mates do anything they wanted as long as they gave me the pleasure I so desperately desired from them.

Emrhys' hand slid to the back of my head to keep me in place as he let himself lose control. When his legs began to shake, I knew he was getting close. To help him along, I allowed my moans to hum around his cock and looked up into his eyes.

"Fuck, princess. This mouth is fucking intoxicating," he said in a moan as his arm began to shake, barely able to keep his hold on my head.

Then come down my throat, daddy.

He grabbed my hair and a guttural groan left his lips as he spilled his salty cum down my throat, just as I'd requested. His cock jerked a couple times against my tongue, dripping the last bit of his cum across my tongue, before he finally pulled out and brought his lips to mine.

Chapter Twenty-Two

Cassiel

Amareon kissed up and down my neck, pounding into my ass at a relentless pace. Between the fullness he was providing, the toe curling spot he was hitting inside—that I wasn't aware existed—and Anevae's cunt milking my cock, I was amazed I hadn't already orgasmed. Anevae had already come once, and the sounds escaping her made me think she was working on another.

After Emrhys came in her mouth, he pulled out and leaned down to kiss her. Then he urged her to sit up. My thrusts stopped, unsure if we'd be able to continue in that position. To my surprise, the way her legs were situated made it so she was basically riding me from the front, and even though I had to sit up more, Amareon adjusted with me.

Anevae rolled her hips, reminding me I'd stopped my movements, and I brought one of my hands to her throat. I pulled her back flush to my front and squeezed her throat lightly. "Keep doing that, and

I'm not going to last long at all. I want one more orgasm from you," I growled low in her ear.

"Then I suggest you continue fucking me," she said as she gripped my arm and rolled her hips again.

"You might be the death of me after all," I grumbled and thrust up into her hard.

Her head fell back against my shoulder as her mouth fell open on a silent scream, and I continued at the punishing pace. Then I watched, entranced, as she released my arm and slipped her hand between her thighs to strum her clit. But Emrhys redirected her hand to the nape of his neck as he swooped in and sucked one of her nipples into his mouth. She tangled both her hands in his hair, pulling him closer.

Emrhys released Anevae's nipple and kissed up to her ear, making her writhe against me. When he reached her ear, he took the lobe between his teeth and tugged on it before whispering, "Do you think you can take two cocks in your needy pussy?"

Anevae's pulse skipped under my fingers, but she didn't say anything; she just stared open-mouthed at the ceiling. My movements faltered, and so did Amareon's behind me. We all waited on bated breath for her to answer him.

"I've never tried something like that. Won't it hurt?" she asked quietly.

"It'll sting at first, but once your body adjusts, you're going to love it. If it becomes too much, we'll stop," he reassured her.

She took a deep inhale and then said, "Fuck it; let's try it."

Amareon's cock twitched in my ass, and I groaned. He kissed my neck with an unspoken apology but grumbled, "Fuck, that sounds like my type of fun and I'm missing out on it. I call dibs next time. Actually, I call being the next one to fuck her pussy."

I elbowed him hard, and he grunted.

Emrhys' lips spread into a teasing smile before he captured her lips and moved closer. One of his hands slithered between Anevae's legs and played with her clit, which had her squeezing me tighter. Then, his fingers probed her tight cunt, skimming the surface of my shaft, and gathered some of her arousal so he could coat his cock with it.

When Emrhys' lips left hers, he whispered, "Ready, princess?" She nodded, panting again, and one of his hands gripped her chin. "You'll tell me if we need to stop, right?"

She forced a rough swallow below my hand and said, "Yes, daddy."

"Fuck, I love it when you call me that," he gritted out.

"Well, get in here before these other two grow soft on us."

I squeezed Anevae's throat slightly tighter. "As long as you're in sight, doing the things you're fucking best at, my cock will never grow soft. Especially when you're naked and your pussy is constantly contracting around me."

She rolled her hips tentatively and sighed at the friction it caused. "Gods, you feel so good. I'm not sure how it's going to feel with both of you in there, but I'm dying to know."

"You're going to love it. Eyes on me, baby." Biting his lip, Emrhys nudged the tip of his cock against my length and eased into Anevae's pussy.

Anevae arched her back, inhaled sharply, and tried to slam her eyes shut, but Emrhys hissed, "Eyes on me," again before sliding in more.

Loosening my grip on her throat, I brought my free hand around to play with her clit and whispered, "Relax, sweetheart."

Behind me, Amareon added, "Breathe through the burn. You're doing so well, pup."

Her body relaxed as she got used to the extra fullness, and her breaths came in slow, measured increments. Once Emrhys was fully seated in her, she was spread so damn tight my cock felt like it was being strangled.

"How does that feel, princess? Are you okay?" Emrhys asked. Anevae nodded, but Emrhys shook his head. "I need the words."

"My pussy feels so full. I need one of you to move. *Please.*"

Emrhys looked over her shoulder at me and Amareon. "Cass, we'll need to alternate at first. Pretty boy, take it easy on the angel's ass until we get a steady rhythm going. We can't risk hurting Anevae right now."

190

Amareon nodded, and Emrhys' eyes locked onto mine. Carefully, he pulled out and slid back in. Anevae's gasp and subsequent moan spurred me on. I followed Emrhys' cautious movements, but they also had me rocking back and forth on Amareon. Unintentionally, I pressed harder on Anevae's clit, which had her clenching harder around Emrhys and I. We both groaned, but continued, our thrusts increasing in speed and ferocity as we went.

When Emrhys finally released Anevae's chin, she threw her head back against my shoulder. Her mouth hung open on scream after scream. She was getting close, but so was I. My balls had drawn so tight they physically ached.

"Em, bite her. I want her to come before I do," I demanded in a moan.

Emrhys wrapped his arms around our girl, and I released her throat. He kissed her neck a couple of times and then sank his teeth into her. Anevae's entire body went rigid as a scream erupted from her, and she constricted so fucking tight around Emrhys and me, coating us in her arousal.

I followed shortly after. The feel of her tightening cunt mixed with Amareon hitting the perfect spot in my ass shoved me off the metaphorical cliff.

When Emrhys retracted his fangs from Anevae's neck, he growled out a loud, "Fuck," and thrust his hips a few more times. He let out another guttural groan as his cum coated her pussy and my cock.

Amareon was the last one left. He pumped into me a few more times with so much force that every time his hips met my ass, the slapping sound of our skin echoed in the room, and I was thrusting into Anevae again. When his hands tightened their grip on my hips and he began shaking, I knew he was getting close. His nails dug into the skin of my hips as he finally filled my ass with his cum.

"We need to do that again sometime because that was fucking amazing," Anevae said.

"I'm trading places with Cassie next time. I want your sweet cunt, Speaking of, I'm going to clean myself off quickly and then will be doing as I promised—cleaning off Cassiel's dick and devouring Anevae's pussy like it's my last meal," Amareon said before pulling out of my ass.

The stretching burned when he first entered me, but gods it felt so good afterward. Wrapping my arms back around Anevae's belly, I pulled her as flush against me as I could with Emrhys' arms also wrapped around her. When she settled back, Anevae's walls fluttered around my cock, making it spring to life again.

"We're all fucking insatiable," I grumbled.

Amareon came up on the bed beside us with a wide smile. "We sure are. Emrhys, go clean off."

"You don't want to clean me up, too?" he asked, feigning hurt.

Amareon raised an eyebrow at the vampire. "I didn't think you'd be into that, but I gladly will if that's what you want."

Emrhys rolled his eyes. "I'm only kidding. I'm not especially into males–just women for me."

"That's what I thought. Now, go," Amareon said, shooing him off.

"You realize you're still going to be cleaning Emrhys off Cassiel, and he's also inside me, right?" Anevae asked.

Once Emrhys was off the bed, Amareon gestured for Anevae to come to him. When she slid off my semi-hard dick, it was like torture. I just wanted her again, actually, as many times as I could have her in a row.

"Gods, you're so beautiful," Amareon said as she went to him.

"I love that all three of you tell me that so often. I've always hated my body," she said.

Amareon grasped the nape of her neck and pulled her mouth to his. They shared a romantic kiss that only made my dick harder as I watched them.

When they separated, he said, "Lay down so I can worship your beautiful body a little more and devour your delectable cunt."

Heat crept across her cheeks as she lay down between Amareon and me. Once she was comfortable, Amareon kissed down her body, wasting little time to get to her pussy. He licked up her slit with an appreciative hum before diving right in.

I watched with rapt attention as she writhed and moaned again. Her hands tangled in his blonde hair, and his gripped her hips. In no time, she was screaming with another orgasm. He licked her through it until she was shoving him away.

He rose on his haunches, licking every ounce of her arousal off him. "Such a good girl. Why don't you join Emrhys in the bathroom to get ready to leave while I take care of our angel?"

My rock hard dick bobbed at that suggestion. Anevae got up and kissed Amareon before she scurried off to join Emrhys. Then Amareon's eyes were on me.

❦ ❦ ❦

While Anevae and Emrhys were in the bathing chamber, Amareon took care of me as he'd promised. When we were done, we focused on cleaning up the room because the carriage was likely already waiting for us. When Emrhys had one commissioned earlier in the day, we hadn't originally planned on the not-so-little rendezvous that happened with all of us. But I was quickly learning that any of Anevae's mates—myself included—would bend over backward to give her whatever she wanted.

After Anevae and Emrhys finished, I dragged Amareon into the bathing chamber behind me. We made quick work of getting ready and rejoined the other two in record time. Anevae had already dug into the food Emrhys and Amareon brought before our literal fuck fest, which made me happy. With as much energy as she'd used the day prior, along with her lengthy rest and the blood she'd lost when Emrhys fed from her, she needed to replenish all the calories she'd lost. Plus, without that food, she'd have a hard time keeping up her energy reserves, too.

Emrhys, Amareon, and I rounded up our things while Anevae finished her food. Amareon and I agreed we'd eat once we got into the carriage because we needed to get going as soon as possible.

The moment Anevae was done, we were off. We were relieved to find the carriage outside, still waiting for us. Emrhys climbed up first and then helped Anevae in. Amareon and I followed, sitting on the bench seat across from them.

When we were finally all settled, Emrhys let the driver know we were ready, and we began our journey to the safe house. I glanced out the window as we began moving, watching the buildings disappear from the small town we left behind.

"How long do we think the trek will take?" I asked.

"Maybe about a day and a half?" Emrhys said.

"Are we weaving back and forth between the territories like we discussed? Or are we trying to get there as soon as possible?" Amareon asked.

"Our first stop is where we planned to retrieve a carriage in the first place, but then we'll take the route we planned on. I'd love to have gone over the plan with the driver, but I don't know this one, so I don't trust him," Emrhys explained.

Amareon nodded, deep in thought, but Anevae's brows were pinched together and her lips were pursed.

"What's going through that pretty little head?" I asked her.

She averted her gaze to Emrhys and asked, "Are you going to be okay traveling in the carriage during the day?"

He leaned over and placed a kiss on her forehead. "I'll be fine, princess. There are shades we can adjust on the windows if needed, and I won't be in direct sunlight, so it'll take longer to hurt me."

Anevae leaned against the carriage's wall and looked out the window. "I hate long trips because I always have so much nervous energy pent up."

"One of us could help you with that if you're interested," Amareon said with a mischievous smile.

I rolled my eyes and smacked his arm. "There isn't nearly enough room in here for that right now."

Anevae's cheeks flushed bright red. "Not completely true. Maeyve and I mated during our carriage ride from Ceraias to Castle Rilvara."

"Neither of you is anywhere near as big as the three of us," Emrhys said.

She shrugged again before leaning her head back. "I'm just saying. Never say never."

My traitorous cock hardened at the thought of her straddling me while the other two watched. I shook my head to clear the thought, but noticed Amareon was sitting eerily still beside me. *Are you okay?*

You sent me that picture and now I can't get it out of my damn head. This is going to be a really long carriage ride, if that's all we can think about, he said.

Amareon was absolutely right... It was a *very* long carriage ride.

Chapter Twenty-Three

Sameera

When Maeyve first told me the madam was her grandmother, I was shocked. I couldn't imagine a grandmother treating her granddaughter that way—my 'grandmother' was different because, well... I was a product of her husband's affair. My relationship with my other grandmother was pleasant, but I didn't see her much growing up, and we never grew close.

But then Maeyve told me who her father was, and I was caught entirely off guard. So much so that I had to take several hours to comprehend how I felt about everything. Every time I looked into her eyes afterward, though, Cahir being her father made sense; the intense orange was the exact same shade as his.

The more I thought about my mate's relation to my personal demon, the less it affected me. She was nothing like him. Every night when she cuddled up to me and every day when she checked on me, her actions told me she was exactly his opposite—a caring and loving woman who would do anything to keep me safe.

Once I came to terms with that, I was more determined than ever to help her take down the madam. That woman had put Maeyve and her mother through so much over the course of Maeyve's life. The bitch didn't deserve to live anymore. In return, Maeyve vowed to help me get revenge on her father and the Lady of Kaeuil.

The first few days after Maeyve's discovery, we tried to learn as much about the madam as possible without her suspecting anything. Maeyve made it a point not to hint at their relation to the madam. But as everyone always said, the woman had eyes and ears everywhere, so we wouldn't be surprised if someone else found out and told her.

I tried not to recommend asking Moranna more about the madam, but we were quickly running out of sources for information by the third day. When I finally asked, Maeyve didn't shut me down like I was afraid, but I could feel the pain creeping through our bond. Because our bond was still so new, we had a hard time blocking each other out most of the time. I loved it—getting to feel close to her even when we were far apart—but she found it cumbersome, especially when she had to see clients. Her first client after our mating made me understand why; the madam hadn't let up on her attempts to make Maeyve submit.

On the night of the third day, Maeyve reluctantly agreed that our best bet for more information was to speak with Moranna, so we went to her room after dinner. Moranna didn't fight with Maeyve when we asked to come in. It was like she knew what was going to happen. To be fair, Maeyve hadn't hidden how much she despised the madam from the beginning, so the fact that we were trying to take her down shouldn't have been a surprise to Moranna.

Moranna directed us toward the couches and said, "I need to get the children to bed before we start. Please help yourself to anything you'd like from the fridge and have a seat."

"I can help you—" Maeyve began.

Moranna shook her head and said, "No. It's okay. I've got them. I'll be back soon."

Maeyve rolled her eyes and led me to the couch. She sat first and then pulled onto her lap, circling her arms around my waist. With one hand across her shoulders, I brought my other to her cheek, but she purposefully looked away.

"What's wrong?" I asked, urging her to look up at me.

"I just want to be out of here—with you and the others who actually care about me. Everyone else can go fuck themselves once we've taken care of our shit," she said.

"We're working on it. Once we get the madam taken care of, we're leaving for that safe house."

"It can't happen soon enough. The only good thing that's come from my time in this place is you," she whispered as a tear escaped her eyes.

I wiped it away and dropped my forehead to hers. "I know, sweetheart."

We sat like that for several minutes, comforting each other in our own ways, while we waited for Moranna. About fifteen minutes later, she finally joined us, sitting on the couch across from ours. In the years I'd known her, she'd never looked as tired as she did then.

"How can I help you, Maeyve?" Moranna asked, point-blank.

"Wow. No, 'hi, how's it going?' I'm impressed. You've always put on the act of a doting mother in front of others. Even when you first got to know Sameera, you made yourself seem like a mom who was wronged," Maeyve said, venom mixing itself into every word.

"There's no changing what I've done. I was trying to protect you, but instead, I put you even further in harm's way. I've done my best to protect every single one of my children since I failed you all those years ago," Moranna explained.

"Glad you learned from your first mistake," Maeyve said as she rolled her eyes. "Anyway, that's not why we're here. I need to know anything you can tell me about Tanith."

Moranna shook her head and sighed. "Vee, you need to be careful with her. She's far more dangerous than you think."

Maeyve scoffed, and her grip on me tightened. "Thanks for the warning. Do you know of any weaknesses she has?"

Moranna took a moment to think about it. "Your father. Ironically, you. Of course, angels. And... mirrors."

"Wait, did you really say mirrors?" I asked, confused.

"Yes. *Mirrors,*" Moranna said, leaning toward us. "Ever noticed how there aren't any in the common areas? Or in some of the guest rooms?"

"No, I haven't," Maeyve said, doing a mental walk-through of the brothel. "Why doesn't she like mirrors?"

"She can't stand to look at her true self," Moranna said, leaning back and crossing her arms.

"What's that supposed to mean?" I asked.

"With her, what you see is not who she is. Tanith has lived for over a millennium, if not two or three. She's done everything she can to maintain the perfect facade of beauty and youth. But when she looks in the mirror, that's not what she sees. She sees the woman who's cut down and attacked those who trusted her; the woman who's taken more lives than any one person can count; and the woman who's taken advantage of those who've had nothing to offer but their own body in exchange for somewhere to live."

"Even more reason to erase her from existence. She's lived far too long," Maeyve mumbled.

"I agree, but remember, with age comes experience," Moranna said.

"Does she have a room in the brothel?" Maeyve asked.

Moranna nodded. "The top floor is her entire suite, but you'll never be able to get up there."

"Does she see clients of her own?" I asked, an idea forming.

"Only high-paying, influential clients."

Turning back to Maeyve, I said, "I have an idea, but we need to talk to the others. We'll likely need their help for this."

Maeyve and I thanked Moranna for her time and headed to our room. She tried to ask questions, but Maeyve ignored her mother flat out. Following her lead, I did the same when Moranna began trying to glean the information from me.

Once we walked out of Moranna's room, Maeyve was in my head, asking questions. *What's your idea? Why do we need to bring our mates into this? How would we even get them to the brothel?*

I shot her a look as we walked and ignored her until we got to our room. Flopping face first on my bed, I said, *Cassiel's an angel, right?*

Yes, he is.

And he has the power of conveyance, right?

He does, but if I remember correctly, angels can't convey themselves to some place they've never been.

Rolling over to look at Maeyve, I asked, *What if we showed him the place we needed him to convey himself to?*

Neither of us is bonded to him, though, Maeyve said, narrowing her eyes on me.

A smile crept across my face. *He's mated to Amareon, though. If I send Amareon my view of the field just outside the city, he can send that same view to Cassiel.*

Well, the madam isn't going to interact with Cassiel, knowing he's an angel, so he won't be able to get close enough to her.

That's why he'd have to bring Amareon along with him. He's a high-ranking, rich fae, and the madam will absolutely go for him. They'd just have to stay in an inn for the night so we can solidify our plan and make sure we haven't drawn too much attention to them.

Maeyve bit the inside of her cheek as she considered my ideas. *Let's talk to the others and see what they think.*

Come sit with me, please. It still hurts to reach out to Amareon sometimes.

Grabbing my hand, she sat on the bed beside me. I whispered a quick thanks before opening my bond with Amareon.

Baby? Can you hear me? I asked.

Kitten? It's so great to hear your voice right now.

It's great to hear yours, too. How are things going over there?

A sense of anxiety trickled through our bond. *Things are going... well.*

Opening up our bond even more, an ache settled in my chest, but it wasn't nearly as bad as it'd been over the past several years. *Where are you?*

His anxiety heightened. *We're almost to the safe house.*

I shot up on the bed and loosened my grip on Maeyve's hand. *Does Maeyve know where you are?*

I don't think she does yet.

Sighing, I watched Maeyve's face closely to see if there were any changes in her demeanor. *No. They haven't. She's not going to be happy, but it's actually good that you guys are already so much closer.*

Oh? Is that so?

Yes. We need your help. Well, yours and Cassiel's help, to be more exact.

Not Emrhys'? He's going to be pissed to hear that you guys don't want his help.

It's not that we don't want his help; it's that the plan we've concocted requires you and Cassiel. Not him or Anevae.

I was about to divulge my plan when Maeyve's mouth fell open and her face went white. "They're in fucking Maiviraea. All four of them."

"Yep. It's kind of good, though. At least Cassiel won't expend as much energy getting him and Amareon to the city."

"As helpful as that is, the first place the king will look for them will be here. Anevae and I are still bonded, and she'll do anything to get me back."

"Well, it's a good thing we're getting out of here soon, then."

"I guess. Have you brought up our plan with Amareon?"

"I was just about to explain it."

"Okay. I'll fill in Anevae and Emrhys. Poor Cassiel will have to wait until we're done."

"I think it'll be fine."

I focused back on my bond with Amareon. *Sorry, baby. They told her where you guys are, and I wanted to make sure she wouldn't act rashly.* Then, I explained our proposed plan to Amareon.

My anxiety grew with each passing minute that I waited for Amareon's response. What if they disagreed with our plan? As badly as Maeyve and I wanted out of the brothel, we had to execute any plan we came up with to perfection.

Cassiel and I are on board. Emrhys, however, is not, he said.

Maeyve's face was fixed into a stern expression, and her anger bubbled through our bond. I placed my hand on her thigh, waiting patiently until she was done speaking to her other mates.

"This has started a bunch of shit and we can't even speak to them all about it together," she said as she shoved herself off the bed and began pacing. Then she turned back to me, jaw clenched, and said, "Fuck this. I don't need their help if it's going to be this much of an issue."

Chapter Twenty-Four

Maeyve

Sameera's eyes widened as I turned and headed for the bathroom. "Maeyve, no!" she yelled after me.

I didn't stop, though. When I made it to the bathroom, I flung the door shut. Sameera caught it just in time, and I whirled around to face her.

She met me head-on, her pink eyes glittering. "What the fuck do you think you're doing?"

"I'm going to face the madam."

Sameera scoffed and crossed her arms over her chest. "You're acting like such a fucking baby right now."

"Excuse me?"

"You're not getting your way, so you're throwing a damn tantrum and putting your life at risk by trying to go after the madam alone."

"Did you not hear what my mom said about the madam's weaknesses? I'm one of them. Mirrors are another. I can fucking do this."

"No. You don't know everything about her. You don't know if she has any special abilities like you do. Get your ass back in the bedroom, take a deep breath and talk to your mates. Make sure Emrhys understands the plan and why it can't be him who helps with it. Don't fucking give up yet."

"You don't know Emrhys. He thinks he can always help."

"You're right, I don't know him. But I *do* know you. Put your foot down and make him listen to you."

"It's not that easy over the bond."

"I beg to differ. Talking about something this important over the bonds allows your mate to feel your emotions—feel how important it is to *you*. If he won't listen, bring Anevae into it more."

"Fine," I grumbled, stomping back to the bedroom and throwing myself onto my bed.

Having effectively shut down my bond, I opened it back up, and Anevae's anger rushed through, hitting me like a brick wall. *What in the fuck, Maeyve? You cannot do that every time we don't agree with you!*

When my anger began to rise, I took a deep breath before I answered. *I'm sorry. I'm just so ready to be done with this place. I miss you guys so fucking much.*

And we miss you too, little fox. Please, let us help you, Emrhys said, voice strained.

Sameera's plan is going to be the best bet. I know you want to help, Em, but we're trying to play into Tanith's weaknesses: me, Cassiel—an angel—and mirrors. Plus, Cassiel needs to be able to get us out of here quickly. The more of us he has to convey, the more energy he'll use. You said that was already hard enough on him when you left the castle. We won't have to travel as far, but still.

Fuck. I don't like not being able to help you, but if this is truly the best plan, we'll make it work, Emrhys said.

Relief washed over me as I looked at Sameera. "Emrhys has agreed to the plan."

A wide smile spread across my mate's face. "Amareon said they should reach the safe house in about an hour or so. They'll reach out once they get there, and I can show them where to go. Cassiel did say he's never done this before, but he thinks it should work."

"Sounds like tomorrow we finally get out of here. And you'll get to see your mate for the first time in far too long."

When Amareon reached out to Sameera later that night, she was able to look out our window at a field in the distance where Cassiel could convey them to. Amareon kept the bond open with her while filtering the image to Cassiel, and we watched the spot on bated breath. Sure enough, a couple of minutes later, Cassiel and Amareon popped up.

Tears sprang to Sameera's eyes, and I wrapped her in a tight hug. "Tomorrow. You'll see him tomorrow."

Once they were securely in the inn just across the street, I dragged Sameera to bed. The next day was going to be a big one. But when we lay down, we tossed and turned, filled to the brim with nervous energy begging to be released.

In the wee hours of the morning, we finally fell asleep. We managed to get a few hours in before we had to get up and ready for the day. While we ate breakfast, Sameera spoke with Amareon, going over the plan one last time.

After eating the last of our breakfast, Sameera and I rounded up our plates. Then we proceeded to the common area just as Amareon strolled through the doors.

One of the girls, a wolf shifter I hadn't had the chance to interact with, rushed forward to greet him. "Hiya, handsome. How can we help you today?"

"Aren't you a cute little thing?" he said, pinching her cheek. "I'd like to speak to the madam of this establishment."

The girl's eyes opened wide. "Whatever for?"

Amareon plastered on a smile I'd only ever thought Emrhys could pull off. "Well, I'm the lord of Eirvanna's son, and I've been sent to Maiviraea for a few events where it's expected that I have a companion. I was hoping the madam could help me find a lovely woman—or two—who can accompany me."

Sameera growled under her breath when the girl clung to him harder and said, "Ooh. The madam is just going to love you. Maybe you can consider letting me join you?"

Meera, be careful. We have to act like we don't know him, I warned.

Averting my gaze, I grabbed Sameera's hand and began pulling her toward the stairs. Her agony shot through her hand into mine, nearly taking me down to the floor, but I refused to stop. Until I heard the madam addressing Amareon.

"How wonderful! Lord Koen's living son in the flesh. I caught a glimpse of you at the ball, but couldn't stay long enough to speak with you and your father. Why don't you join me in my quarters upstairs so we can discuss your needs?"

"Lead the way."

They headed for the main stairs while we were headed to the service stairwell. When we got to our room, Sameera checked in with Amareon and I hauled ass to get dressed. I was hopeful he'd be able to get us into her room before long.

Once Sameera was dressed, we headed for the stairs. We'd made it one flight up before Sameera stopped completely.

What's wrong? I asked.

She's going to be sending someone to retrieve us from our room. We need to go back, she said, turning on her heel to sprint back to our room.

We made it back with a minute to still catch our breath before a servant showed up to escort us to the madam's quarters. We followed, but when we were nearly there, I realized I'd forgotten something—a mirror. There wouldn't be one up in the madam's quarters, and I couldn't stop somewhere to get one.

Tell Amareon that Cassiel needs to bring a mirror. We didn't have one in our room besides the one built into the bathroom wall, and I wasn't about to go breaking it.

She nodded and went quiet, passing the message to Amareon. When we reached the last set of stairs, my heart rate spiked. This could easily all go wrong, and the last thing I wanted was someone to get hurt. If they did, I'd blame myself for the rest of my life.

The servant approached the door, knocked, and waited for the madam to grant us access. As Sameera and I entered, the madam introduced us both, but didn't hide her disdain for me. Amareon surprised me when he rose from his chair and approached Sameera.

Meeting her gaze, he picked up her hand and placed a gentle kiss on her knuckles. "It's a pleasure to meet you, Sameera."

Her cheeks flushed a bright red, but she didn't move. "It's a pleasure to meet you as well, sir."

After placing another kiss on Sameera's hand, he came to stand in front of me. Reaching down, he picked up my hand, and a jolt of electricity zapped up my arm. I forced myself to stay still, not wanting to betray our relationship.

He brought my knuckles to his lips, kissing them ever so lightly. "You said this one is Maeyve, correct?"

"Yes. She's my biggest troublemaker. I'm not sure why you'd be interested in her."

"Maybe I'm looking to cause a little bit of mayhem. One will never know for sure."

The madam just hummed in response.

Releasing my hand, he winked at me and turned to face the madam. "How about we discuss cost?"

The madam opened her mouth to speak just as Cassiel appeared in the chair Amareon had been seated in, and Sameera darted toward the door. She quickly locked it as the madam watched, mouth agape.

"What the fuck is going on? And who the fuck are you?" the madam asked Cassiel.

I stepped out from behind Amareon and strolled up to the madam. "We're about to have a heart-to-heart. *Grandmother.*"

"Ah. It seems your mother has finally informed you of who I am. I was beginning to wonder how long it would take her."

A loud smack echoed through the room when the back of my hand connected with her cheek. "You're a despicable being, and I think you need a reminder of just how awful you are. Cass," I said, beckoning him forward.

He placed the mirror in my hand and moved behind the madam to restrain her. "Do you want to know who I am?" he asked as he spread his black wings. "My name is Cassiel, and I will be your undoing."

About the author

Mikaelynn Rose is a hard-working, devoted woman whose world revolves around an amazing little boy... well, I guess her husband, too. While she lives just outside of Denver with her high school sweetheart and son, she'd much rather be in the country or the mountains. When she's not working, she's writing, reading, listening to music, spending time with her loved ones, and, of course, drinking way too much coffee for her own good.

Find me on my socials!

f facebook.com/mikaelynnrose/

♪ tiktok.com/@mikaelynnrose

♪ tiktok.com/@author.mikaelynn.rose

◉ instagram.com/mikaelynnrose

g goodreads.com/mikaelynnrose